Faithful Brothers?

A Novel

D1522826

Courtney Alexander Williams

First published by Dog Ear Publishing
4010 W. 86th Street, Ste H
Indianapolis, IN 46268
www.dogearpublishing.net

ISBN: 978-145750-610-9

This book is printed on acid-free paper.

Printed in the United States of America

To Una Williams, my Grandmama,
who told me I could do anything
when I followed her words and ways—
and manners

ACKNOWLEDGMENTS

This story of leaving Africa partly grows out of my experience of living like an adopted son with a family in Senegal, Africa. My name there is Mussa Ndao (literally "Moses King"). It also springs from my own coming to America. These transitions tested the ideas and training that my grandmother, Una Williams, gave me.

I would first like to extend my gratitude to Oprah Winfrey for 25 years of her show, which touched and healed many broken lives around the world, including mine. The number of people who shared their life stories of overcoming different obstacles in life—these had a real impact on me. In more than a few ways, people were encouraged not to give up or give in on their dreams. For the past five years, Oprah has inspired me to preserver and complete this book. With this, from the bottom of my heart, I give kudos and thanks, and many blessings of success to you, Oprah, and your staff.

I also want to extend my gratitude to Virginia Bell, Pastor Kofi, Trooper McKenney, Hermin Cherrington, Kellie Cameron, and Timothy Staveteig.

To become an actor, I want to acknowledge the faculty of the Connecticut School of Broadcasting and the School for Film and Television in New York.

Since 1998, I have been a member of the Screen Actors Guild (SAG) and American Federation of Television and Radio Artists (AFTRA), and since 2002, a member of Actors' Equity (AEA). Although I live in and around the New York City area, I have also trained in Los Angeles. Many other members, directors, and assistants have helped shape my acting abilities, especially after performing in over a dozen movies, nearly a dozen television programs, and half-dozen Off-Broadway theatre productions.

Aspects of this story were researched, and I want to thank Barbara Satow for her efforts in making several elements plausible and not out of character with the times.

This book is dedicated to my Grandmother, Una Williams, who told me I could do anything when I followed her ways of wisdom and manners. Her teachings in my young life made my transition into adulthood smoother.

Finally, I want to give honor to God. The struggle between Abdalla and Chijioke is an updated version of the Parable of the Prodigal Son, with a twist—that both brothers leave home to explore new worlds and that father and family joins them in place and celebration; neither brother returns home. Just like the elder brother in the parable, however, Abdalla is not requited for his diligence and steadfastness.

CHAPTER

1

My name is Abdalla Ndao, and I know the very day in 1970 when I began sprinting away from my father's farm to capture life in a new land. My younger brother, Chijioke, and I are up early as the Saturday morning sun is clearing the horizon. We are still in our grass hut in our village, not too far from our fields. We go out the doorway still getting our jeans buttoned.

Each of us grabs a hoe, and on this morning, I challenge my brother to a race to the fields. At first, he declines because, he says, he will easily win. Then he charges away first; my start is late, and I run as fast as I can. Yet this day I win the race.

Such a race, of course, is silly as I look back. That, however, is not the reason it stands out in my memory. Nor do I recall this day because I beat him. This day stands out because I realized how a foot race captures the competition between us—we are so close in age and strength—and how Chijioke's trick-start depicts the different ways we approach life. I can have a slow start or take the extra steps. Yet Chijioke looks for the caper—the capricious escapade and its playful prance. That day, I won the prize.

***

Arriving at the field in such a rush, Abdalla and Chijioke needed to catch their breaths; each was hunched over and panting. The morning breeze still carried coolness, and Abdalla turned his face to catch it. Even so, his face felt as if a warm soaked cloth were wiping it, melting his eyes and smothering his nostrils. Abdalla gasped, waiting for this feeling to pass.

"Do you ever think of America, Chijioke?" Abdalla asked.

"All the money those people have," Chijioke replied. "It must be nice to be rich."

Chijioke's mind drifted to another scene, his image of America. Rich meant staying at home in the shade—no doubt with a cool drink that captured the humidity in rivulets of moisture slipping down the glass. It meant savoring the sweet, gentle smells. Here the sun was now well above the horizon, and the day's heat had begun. The heat smelled sweaty, even sticky as his nose scrunched up to filter it out. All the coolness from the early morning at the hut was being pushed out, lost, as he panted, exhaling and inhaling.

Abdalla and Chijioke lifted their heads and eyed each other as if in agreement. The race had made this hoeing chore even more burdensome for a Saturday. No one had really won.

Abdalla focused his eyes to survey the job ahead—hoeing weeds from the peanut rows. Against the red brown earth, these green peanut plants were a vivid contrast in color, but not smell. Already the plants had curled their leaves. In the early morning, they smelled like red vinegar, sweet at first and then delivering a pungent tang like an onion. Their scent always put a taste on the tongue that was fresh and then slightly bitter. Even the plants, Abdalla thought, were bent over, bracing themselves for the scorching day.

Peanuts could sustain the Ndao family after most of the produce was sold, provided that Abdalla and Chijioke would keep the plants alive and productive. Peanuts needed a little more moisture than a typical year of rainfall in southern Senegal would provide. Yet for the past few years, droughts plagued the region, making the situation desperate. The earth could not retain enough moisture from the wet and cold rainy season to outlast the dry and smothering hot season. The heat could be so treacherous, reaching across Senegal into Casamance, southern Senegal, which is only a short distance from the Sub-Sahara.

In a good year, the typical farm income was about $130; Senegal was second only to Nigeria in the export of peanuts and peanut oil. Thanks to the World Bank and *Programme Agricole*, their father had been able to get seed, fertilizer, and simple equipment, like the hoes, on credit in exchange for the return of the seed plus 25 percent of the remaining harvest. In recent years, however, giving back so much of the produce meant that the cash crop did not produce enough cash for the family.

The two brothers walked between the crop rows. When one came upon a weed, he would plant the hoe tip behind the weed's stem and flick it out into the sun. Weeds that might steal moisture could not be tolerated.

The top of the red soil had already been baked dry so that crust kept the sun from reaching down further into the soil. The two brothers tried not to stir that crust with their hoeing because doing so would expose any moisture under the surface to be baked away. Presently the balance was held, but each knew that the heat could crack open the ground as the dry top soil descended deeper and deeper.

The conversation between the brothers was not hurried. They had miles to walk and weed and work up things to say.

"Not everyone is rich in America," Abdalla reply to Chijioke.

"It doesn't seem that way to me," he retorted.

"I hear it's beautiful."

"Forget that. What about all the money those people have?" Chijioke spite back.

More steps and movements of the hoe. Then Abdalla answered, "Is money all you think about?"

"Yeah," his brother replied, "It's better than living here."

"But we are helping mom and dad in the field," Abdalla said.

It felt odd that Chijioke didn't realize how old their parents had gotten and how much they count on their children to help out.

Chijioke laid down on the red soil between the rows, propping his chest up by leaning on one elbow, while arranging the other hand as though he held a refreshing drink.

"I'd rather be lying by a pool, sipping the latest and tastiest cold alcoholic drink."

This puzzled Abdalla.

"You've had alcohol before?" he asked.

"No, but I can imagine what it tastes like; it tastes rich and cold and...and...may I have some more, please?"

"Oh, okay," Abdalla said.

He lay down in the field in the next row over.

"I can see myself in America making movies. That's my dream."

He thought back to the first movie he'd seen, *The Greatest Story Ever Told*. The missionaries played in on an old projector. It retold the story of Jesus, from the Nativity through the Resurrection. Yet somehow, Abdalla had become more intrigued by the movie-making than the movie's message. He was in love with great stories, big stories, presented on a big screen.

Chijioke continued, "I can see myself in America because I want an easy life."

"So forget hard work?"

"Yes."

"I know that making movies will start off as hard work," Abdalla said, sticking with his own dream, "but I'm sure it will get easier."

Yes, he thought, hard work and a life of ease shouldn't remain as opposites. Some path must exist to merge his epic movie life and his brother's dream to have an easy life.

"It must be something, going to fancy luncheons, meeting important people, going to parties," he ventured.

Yes, perhaps parties would be the meeting place for the two.

"Parties," Chijioke said, stretching out the word and laughing while he said it. "Par-ti-es, now you're talking." He thought, *I want my nights to be parties, and my days to be recuperation.*

"What it is all about, I don't know," Abdalla admitted. "I want to work so hard that someday I can win some kind of award."

"Sure you will," Chijioke chortled, scoffing at the idea of hard work being required.

It seemed obvious to him that two paths were set before each young adult: the way of his parents who had worked hard, but who attained an existence only step ahead of a bad crop year; and the way of the rich who do as they please away from the hot fields.

"I will someday," Abdalla insisted.

"Yeah, yeah, yeah. But you are only human. So be sure to thank your family," Chijioke snickered.

"I will," Abdalla promised, "especially you."

"Right, especially me."

The brothers laughed at this, until they heard their father, Issa, in the field. He yelled, "Hey, boys, get off your butts and get to work!" Issa also had a hoe and had begun working on his own row. The brothers jump up and wiped their pants as they got back to work again.

***

In the native language, the word for "house" and "family" was the same. A village was configured in family groupings or compounds fenced off with vegetation such as millet stalks, thorns, or palm fronds. Inside the compound, each family's hut opened to a central court-yard. Before Christian missionaries came, the family head had his own hut that he shared with his elder sons. Each wife had her own hut, which she shared with her younger children. Unmarried sons or older women might be given their own huts. And a newly married son would be given a hut for himself and his wife, sectioned off within the compound.

That arrangement had stopped many years ago. The missionaries had encouraged men to marry only one wife and live with her in one hut with children until the children could move out to a single's hut of young men or women. At first, the singles or the newly married could take one of the previously built huts. But long before Abdalla and Chijioke were born, Issa had built the family hut in their family area. By the time the girls were walking and playing, he had needed to build a second hut, simply abandoning the first. Thus, each family village was a hodge-podge of active and vacant huts, often in decline.

The Ndao hut was built of grass thatches for the roof and wall coverings. The walls had been back plastered with fresh mud on both the inside and outside. Openings had been left for sunlight and breezes along the top of the walls, and a doorway opening for entering and exiting. In the northern area, most huts were round. Among the Casamance, however, the huts tended to be rectangular in shape with the door at one of the narrower ends. This permitted an entrance area leading into a vestibule before the main room. The vestibule was used for eating, and it contained their earthen bowls to process as well as the day's food supply along with pots. The main room held their sleeping platform shared by all inhabitants with a mat or animal hide to cover for the night.

Drawing in a lung-full of air, one could catch a whiff of the grass's lemon-nutty smell. The floor was packed dirt that felt cool to bare feet, especially on a warm day. The Ndao's three daughters sat on the floor for their Bible instruction. In front of them was their mother, Suma, who wanted to finish their lesson before moving back to chores.

"And God will supply all your needs, according to His riches in glory," Suma concluded. "How many times have we seen God supply our needs?" she asked.

Abimbola, the third child and oldest daughter, gave the quick answer, "Many times."

"Abimbola, can you remember any time God supplied our needs?" her mother questioned.

"Dad broke his foot in the field," Abimbola started out rather slowly as if she were constructing the scene in her mind, and then finished rapidly. "So we had to work, and it was talked about in the villages, and many people came to bring in the harvest." Abimbola was relieved because her lesson was now completed.

"Yes, that is right," Suma said. "Amia, what do you remember?"

Amia, the middle daughter, said confidently, "I prayed for a doll and God supplied one for me."

"So God supplies our wants, too. How about you, Aba?"

Aba, the youngest daughter, replied, "I prayed for a Bible, and the missionaries got one for me, and they taught me English to read it."

"They taught us all English," Suma replied, "That is why you girls go to school. Well, we'd better stop for today and get ready for lunch."

After putting away their Bibles, Suma stepped outside to a fire pit where meat was slowly cooking. Although barely midday, she also felt as though she was slowly cooking in the sun's flames. A trickle of sweat came down her cheek, then another down her neck and onto her simple dress.

Meanwhile, Abimola, Amia, and Aba. got lunch ready for the family. Aba, the youngest, put a table-cloth down on the floor and smoothed out its wrinkles until completely flat. Amia got down one big bowl and start filling it with rice, peanuts, and vegetables. Suma would add the chicken and fish as soon as it was ready. And Abimola carefully poured water into another large bowl, the one the family used for washing hands.

The men enter the hut, and Abimola balanced the bowl of water while carrying it to their area. The men washed and dried their hands and wrists, and then took their places on the floor.

Suma also walked into the hut, carrying a platter filled with chicken and fish. She and Aba carefully added this bounty to the large bowl of food. What a rich fare, Suma thought, enough to feed the entire family.

Before leading the family in a prayerful thanks to God, Issa surveyed the bounty of food before them. The smells so mingled with one another, but he thought he could pick out each one. How good to be back from the fields. How good to have the work finished before Sunday. How good to be so well off.

CHAPTER

2

The hazy cigarette smoke lit up as a shaft of light centered on a young woman seated on a stool on the stage. She scanned the Saturday-night crowd seated around small tables with white cloths. Some were sipping drinks, others talking quietly, and a few finishing or starting cigarettes. Where's the music? she wondered. She turned, not to the DJ, but to Feury's table. Tonight she wanted only to sing to him, to sing for him. This could be her break, he had set it up, and she expected everything to be smooth.

Feury, owner of Feury's Alley Jazz Club, caught her gaze, and he smiled at her, lifting his drink a bit to toast her before taking a sip. Aha, the taste of de-fizzed Coca-Cola in a glass for red wine. To others it looked like one of the dark local vintages, but this little charade kept him sharp and alert. Well, that and discovering local singers. When she made it on the world's stage—this wasn't a question of if in his mind—she would connect his club to all the other hot clubs.

The women next to the owner ignored what was going on. Two were chatting, one was extinguishing a cigarette, and another was talking with a music agent in an Italian suit who had just been seated. Two obvious body guards, arms crossed as they scanned the crowd, looked like jacks in a royal court that included the singer.

The singer then turned to the DJ, and the music instantly came up; a soft jazz number. She leaned into the microphone, and her raspy, throaty sound quieted the crowd. Feury surveyed his empire and smiled. The club was magic again tonight. He could be anywhere in the world, but he was here, at home.

The music made his mind wander. So many places for African Americans were much farther North in Harlem, but they featured Dixie Land jazz. Louis "Satchmo" Armstrong was well-known for this style, but he had died a couple of years prior, and Feury thought that this style was waning. No, his club in Greenwich Village offered a place to enjoy music without going to a more formal club with cover charges and dress codes. When Feury had come to the U.S., he turned his African talents on the drums into "free jazzing" with John Coltrane. Feury loved the melting pot of jazz styles he had created here, especially when he was able to book an avant-garde band from Europe and Japan. He farmed out talent to scouts whenever he could—for a commission, of course. For the pretty good musicians and singers, he had formed a recording label, Endurance Records, to capture their early sounds and help promote them.

Only one thing need happen, Feury thought, to close a great spot: the invasion of the outside world puncturing a club's inner world, like fresh air being fanned in and pushing out the smoky haze. Trumpeter Lee Morgan came to mind. His common law wife had shot him to death last year over at Slug's in the East Village. Now that establishment was struggling. Death's reality had cleared the air in a little corner of paradise.

When the singer finished, the crowd clapped and turned to its other distractions. Feury bent in the direction of the music agent.

"How about that? She sings like an angel," he crooned.

"She's really good, Feury. Where did you find her?"

"She works for me here at the club. She is one of my waitresses, and she said she wanted one chance to sing. One of our regulars called out sick, and she replaced him. She's been singing ever since."

"What's her name?"

"Beth Myer."

The music agent turned to look at Beth and started to get up. "If you don't mind, I am going to have to talk to Beth Myer. Maybe I can get her a contract deal."

Feury gently laid his hand on top of the agent's hand and said, "That is why I wanted you to come tonight. I was hoping you can help her with her career in the business."

The agent's attention seemed already drawn away by some attractive force, no longer present with Feury, as the agent moved toward Beth Myer on that small stage.

Feury hardly noticed as he settled back into his booth seat between the women seated under his arms. He took another sip from his wine glass and ran his tongue over his lips. Feury loved the taste of thick cigarette smoke when it settled on everything. It whispered that patrons were here watching, drinking in the sounds, and enjoying themselves. "Perhaps I should have called this the 'Blue Haze Club.' But my, do I love this business," he mumbled to himself.

CHAPTER

3

The royal red and gold of the Ndao clan in their traditional African dress gleamed in the early Sunday morning sun. Already Abdalla and Chijioke were at the road, which led to the church. Then the three girls walked in a group, approaching the road, several feet behind their brothers. Finally, Suma with Issa in one hand and her Bible in the other, walked behind the girls.

The family's hut compound was on the edge of their village. The roadway passed another compound on the right with its family collection of huts. Then Amia turned around walking backward and asked, "Mother, are we going to have another Bible lesson from the missionary today?

"Yes, I believe so."

"Abdalla," Issa called ahead, "I think you are going to enjoy this, the missionary who is visiting today is from the United States. He is from a church in New York City."

Abdalla stopped kicking stones and halted. "Really, dad?" he asked.

He was half-thinking his father was teasing, half-hoping the news was true.

"Yes," Issa replied. "We know that you always talk about someday going to the U.S. and studying there."

Abdalla said with a tremble, "Do you think he can help me find a school to go to?"

"I don't know, I hope so."

Suma released Issa's hand and stepped forward reaching to touch Abdalla.

"We did not want to tell you he was coming until we knew he was actually here. He's here for two weeks. After that, he is flying back to the U.S. You should talk to him."

Abdalla missed his mother's gesture and turned to slap his hand against Chijioke's in a show of triumph.

They walked on the road in silence. They passed a village of empty huts. An outsider might have thought that others were already on their way to the church. Yet the truth was that these families had fled because of government treatment. The Ndao's knew this.

Just then, Abdalla caught the outline of a man by a bush near the road on the left side. The man shifted his weight back-and-forth, from one foot to the other, making soft grunts while holding up a grass reed as though it were a sword.

Abdalla was closest to the man and, when he caught the man's foul smell, he backed away. The man had on a jacket as though it were cold out. He wore a tunic underneath that was wet from spit and greasy from overuse. His hair was matted and his beard, scruffy. Several teeth were missing. His eyes bulged.

They seemed to be opened wider than Abdalla thought normal.

Suma let out a scream, and she and Issa gathered around the girls. Chijioke was so taken back that he stiffened for a moment.

The man took Abdalla's action and closeness as signals to pursue. Abdalla wasn't sure whether to strike the man or run. Then the man lifted his grass reed as if to strike, and Issa called out, "Come on, girls!"

And the man backed away.

Then his muttering became audible.

"There they are all going to church again. Every Sunday they go to church. They think that by going to church, God will bless them," the man said to no one in particular or maybe to himself. He turned to Abdalla.

"Where is God for me?" he pleaded. "God makes me starve."

Then Suma stepped forward toward the man.

"God is right with you," she said. "Call on the Lord's name. God will provide for you."

The man, who had seemed to Abdalla as bewildered, now seemed more focused. He had engagement. His rocking from foot to foot stopped as he took in Suma's words.

"You mean…? You mean, call on…what?" he repeated her words. "No, there is no God."

Amia, the middle daughter, stepped forward around her father.

"Yes, there is."

Issa pulled her back, saying in a loud hissing voice. "Amia, don't talk to this man."

Then she stood up and said plainly, "Go away, old man."

Putting his hand near his head and then swatting the air between him and Issa, the man said, "You are all crazy."

Finally, Chijioke jumped back into action. "No, you're crazy," he called out, pointing his finger at the man.

"Chijioke, don't torment the man," Issa commanded.

"But, he is mean," Chijioke defended.

"He's mean because he's ill," Issa said in exasperation.

"Maybe he feels that God let him down," Suma suggested.

"But what caused him to be ill?" Abimbola asked emphatically.

"He is bitter because he has troubles," her mother assured her.

"But why does God give us hard times?" Abimbola pleaded.

She lowered her tone, "I don't know why. Maybe he did something or he may have been hurt by some tragedy and never got over it."

"Unfortunately, in this life," her father warned, "there will be trouble."

"But God delivers us out of these troubles?" Aba, the youngest daughter, ask for reassurance.

"Right, Aba," her dad said with conviction.

"And God walks us through our trials and gives us peace," Suma said.

With that, the man retreated to an empty hut, and the family continued on their way to worship.

***

The lazy dust lit up as a shaft of sunlight streamed through a small window at apex of the wall in the front of the church building. For a while, the brightness from the window had bothered John Eaton when he sat back behind the podium. At the close of worship, he had marched with the local pastor to the back door to greet the worshipers. As John looked back, he saw that the benches and blackboards could have suggested the shabby white building was a school, but the large cross just below the window marked it as a church. Maybe throughout the week, it served as both. Although the building was neat and well-kept, John thought it was far from his New York congregation and its sanctuary. Even so, he had wanted to do missionary work, and being on site gave him more credibility for raising support.

The sun's angle now at mid-day let a strong shaft of light into the sanctuary. As Abdalla Ndao shuffled toward the exit, that beam caught him in the face; he needed to cup a hand to his left side in order to keep the hot light from his face. Others felt it also, and it pushed some of the congregation toward the doorway. Abdalla tried to take a small step forward, but gentle conversation among the worshipers caused them to sidle a half-step and then stop, another half-step and stop. No one seemed anxious to leave, except Abdalla, who stretched and twisted his arms in various positions, as if he were waking up; then he cupped his hands as though he were about to receive some bread. It was all nerves.

Abdalla's family was with him. His father insisted that they come early to sit near the front. Issa stood behind Abdalla to meet further with

John, the missionary. Issa had staged this moment, and he waited for John to finish shaking hands with others nearby.

"Excuse me, my name is Issa."

Issa stepped around Abdalla, after spotting an opening.

"Hi, Issa. I'm John Easton. It is nice to meet you."

"I wanted to say how encouraged I was by your sermon."

Issa wished he had planned this part better. Should he have said something more specific or insightful? Was he really encouraged by what John said or simply the fact that John was here? What was the sermon text again? Well, he was only human.

"Thank you very much."

John smiled as he finished the handshake, looking into Issa's eyes.

Issa again reached behind Abdalla and moved him forward toward John.

"This is my son Abdalla. Your presence here is an answer to my family's prayers."

That felt better, Issa thought, and it felt true.

"Really?"

John was genuinely surprised at this. He had felt called to raise financial support for new missions in Africa. Yet he hadn't thought his presence was also hoped for here in Africa.

"Our pastor said you went to New York University, NYU."

"Yes, I did."

Again, John looked into Issa's eyes and smiled as again they shook hands.

"I got my degree in communications before I became a pastor."

Issa smiled as though this made perfect sense.

"My son has always wanted to go to United States and study in your country."

Abdalla's fidgeting stopped; his breathing stopped; he stood motionless, as if he were a tree trunk. John turned toward Abdalla.

"What do you want to study?"

Abdalla opened his mouth, but no sounds came out. He cleared his throat.

"I want to make movies."

He spoke in a higher pitch than usual. He hesitated. Should he say more? Perhaps tell John that he had wanted to make movies since he saw his first one?

"Well, then NYU is the school to go to. They have an excellent film department."

"How can I get there?" Abdalla asked.

Did that sound, he wondered, like he was asking for directions? Well, he was asking for specifics—and for help.

"I believe you would have to go through the admissions process for the school and then would need to get a student visa."

Issa now stepped forward a bit. He wanted to ask if John could help him help Abdalla become the success he envisioned? Issa was suddenly aware of the long pause.

"Could you help him with that?"

"I would love to," John said turning back to Abdalla. "I even own an apartment building that I rent to students. If you get accepted, you can stay there."

Abdalla could not contain his excitement.

"That sounds great."

Then he fell silent again. On the inside, however, he was jumping up and down.

John continued, "I want to hear more about this film school dream you have."

Then he turned back to Issa.

"What are you doing later?"

"Whatever you would like to do."

Meeting with John was the most important thing today, Issa thought, and perhaps the most important thing in Abdalla's entire future.

"I have a commitment for lunch with your pastor and his family," John said. "But, let's see if we can sit together so that I can learn more."

John then moved toward others to shake their hands, not signaling—at least not showing—how important this conversation might be.

Meanwhile, Abdalla's expression was beaming, and his excitement made him child-like because he could not believe this turn of events.

"Can we dad? Can we go for lunch?" he said like a ten-year old.

"Certainly," Issa said, looking into Abdalla's eyes.

John turned back and said, "When I go back home, I can send you the information and requirements on becoming a student."

Abdalla and Issa hugged each other with excitement.

"Let's go to lunch," John said.

Then he put one arm around Issa and the other around Abdalla.

***

After the lunch with John and their pastor in his hut and then the hot dusty road home from church, the Ndao's hut with its packed dirt floor felt cool on Abdalla's feet. The other family members followed Abdalla through the hut entrance; Sunday after worship was a day of rest. Abdalla turned to exit, and Chijioke followed.

"Abdalla, where are you going?" Chijioke asked.

"In the field," Abdalla replied.

"Why? It's Sunday. We don't work on Sunday."

"I'm not going to work."

"Why are you going?" Chijioke ran to catch up.

"To pray."

"About what?"

"To thank God for letting me meet the missionary and to ask that the missionary be able to get me to the U.S."

They walked along the path to the field in silence. Upon entry, Abdalla carefully got down on his knees, closed his eyes, and began to pray in earnest.

Chijioke just sat on the ground, scanning the field and then Abdalla. He saw his brother's lips moving, but could not hear what was being said. This was pretty dull, he thought. Wait. He had spotted something shiny, sparkly just peeking out from below the surface of the path.

Moving closer, Chijioke carefully picked up the little stone. He rubbed the red dirt from its surface. His eyes widen. It's a diamond, he screamed in his mind. Had Abdalla seen him? Chijioke slowly turned back toward Abdalla so as not to attract further attention. His brother was still praying, still moving his lips, still closing his eyes, still clenching his hands in front of his chest, still pouring his heart and his dreams out to God.

Good, Chijioke thought. Then keeping his hands and feet on the ground, he slowly lifted his body up and crawled like a crab over to another sparkly spot. More diamonds. Chijioke picked, polished, and poked as many stones into his pants pocket as he could. Then he turned his head to eye his brother. Then he moved to another spot and continued gathering diamonds. This went on for a long time, and for once Chijioke was glad his brother had big, detailed dreams.

Chijioke's discovery was a surprise to him, but not really a shock. Casamance was on the northern edge of the alluvial diamond deposits in western Africa. Chijioke knew that discoveries were accidental, but usually involved an ancient water flow, especially flowing northward.

The diamonds were near the surface and could be mined by persons with a shovel and a diamond pan. Some material was placed in the pan, which was then filled with water. Swirling and tipping it to one side near the riffles allowed some sediment to escape. With a bit of luck, one would find a few diamonds at the bottom.

Chijioke had tried his hand at this several times, but never with success. Like taking a boy fishing, if he had caught one or two early on, he might have stay at diamond hunting longer. But, it was hot, tiring work, especially when the effort went unrewarded.

But now look here! Chijioke thought. Here they were practically on the surface of the ground; no dipping or swirling needed. Just pick them up and rub them off. This was how Chijioke had dreamed life would be.

Something changed, and Chijioke looked over at Abdalla. "All this I ask in your name, dear God …," Abdalla prayed. Chijioke heard this and skillfully moved into a kneeling prayer posture, clutching his hands in front of his chest.

"Amen," Abdalla said in great relief.

"Amen," Chijioke said.

His relief was equal to Abdalla's because Chijioke had picked up many diamonds without being observed. He was on the road to a care-free life.

Each brother got up from his knees to walk home, thankful for what he had received.

"Can you imagine me studying in the U.S. at New York University?" Abdalla asked.

"That's great," Chijioke replied.

He was thinking more about his own future than Abdalla's.

"That's just great," he repeated.

CHAPTER

4

Monday's work was delayed in the morning because of hot winds. Abdalla had stayed in the hut to do reading for his assignments. Chijioke, in contrast, had decided to take a walk into the town a couple of miles away. Even though this seemed like more effort than Chijioke usually applied, his parents were pleased that he was pursuing something. He had returned before lunch.

By early afternoon the Ndao family was able to return to their hoeing in the fields. To get their work done, the entire family had worked. Other villagers had also waited and were in their fields as families. By late afternoon, the girls were tired, and Suma thought it was time to make the evening meal.

"I'm going to take the girls back to the hut to prepare for supper," Suma said to Issa as she stopped hoeing.

Issa stood upright from his bent hoeing position and nodded his head.

"Girls," he said, "I want you to go and help your mother to get supper ready."

"Yes, father," Abimbola and Aba said in unison.

"Yes, Dad," Amia the middle daughter said, seeking her own voice.

The girls and Suma walked home and began their usual routine. Amia mixed couscous; Abimbola shucked the peanuts from their shells; and Aba washed the vegetables. Suma moved to the fire pit to stir up its few embers in order to cook the meal's meat. Unlike the girls who enjoy the shade and coolness of the hut, Suma stood in the later afternoon's hot sun and over the hot fire pit. As was often true, her face beaded with sweat. She dabbed off the sweat beads with a handkerchief.

She finished her cooking as the men return from the field, and the Ndao family gathered inside. Aba got the washbasin and towel, and handed these to her father so that he and the brothers could wash their hands.

As they finished their supper, they heard a knock at the hut entrance. Issa turned to Suma and said in a whisper, "Who is that?"

"I don't know," she replied.

"I mean, were you expecting anyone?"

"No, were you?"

Issa cleared his throat and, without standing up, spoke in a loud voice.

"Can I help you?"

An official, authoritative voice sounded back.

"I am looking for Issa Ndao."

Issa got up from the floor, walked over toward the entrance to peer outside. Some sort of government official was at the doorway. Other military men were sitting in the back of a Jeep. Taken back, Issa nevertheless moved to the doorway.

"These are for you," the official said.

He shoved some documents into Issa's face.

"What are these papers?"

Issa attempted to swat them from his face as though they were bothersome flies.

"We are here to inspect your land," the official said.

"What? Inspect? Why? ..."

Issa fumbled for words for a situation he cannot grasp. All he could think was that this was highly unusual. Perhaps there was a mistake. Or, something had gone terribly wrong.

"Ask your son," the official bellowed.

Letting the papers fall to the floor, the official turned on his heels and walked toward the field.

Officials from Senegal were hated. The people of the Casamance had remained with Senegal when it achieved its independence in the 1960s. The agreement had been that Casamance would achieve its independence within 20 years. But the Senegalese had extracted heavy penalties and abused the peasants in this region.

Now the officials had come to the Ndao family.

Issa stepped outside the doorway and saw several trucks with men unloading shovels. The men also threw out empty buckets from the trucks into the field.

Issa screamed, "Abdalla! Chijioke! Come here! Now!"

The brothers ran from the vestibule to Issa, standing in the doorway.

"What is this man talking about?"

"Dad, what is going on?" Abdalla asked.

"These men are here to inspect my land! What is this man talking about?"

"I don't know, dad," Abdalla said.

He was as confused as his father.

Chijioke shrugged his shoulders and looked away. Issa caught his nonchalance.

"Chijioke, what did you do today?" Issa spit out.

"I-I-I didn't do anything. I just went to town," Chijioke defended.

Issa picked up the papers to inspect them.

"Why, they're not here to inspect my land. They're here to take my land. How could this happen? What do they know?"

"I don't know, dad," Abdalla repeated.

"Chijioke, what have you done?"

Issa shouted as he grabbed Chijioke by the T-shirt he was wearing.

"I-I-I found some diamonds in the field, and I sold them."

"Who told you they were diamonds?" Issa demanded.

"The men I sold them to," Chijioke defended. "They were on the ground, I picked them up."

He thought for a moment, then continued.

"You told us they were shiny rocks. I just wondered if they were more."

"Where did you sell the diamonds?"

"I went to the city and found men who looked like they had money."

Issa let Chijioke go, and then he rubbed his forehead as if to sooth a headache.

"When did this happen?"

"This morning, when we were waiting for the weather to change," Chijioke said softly.

Sensing that he could mollified his father's anger, he walked through the vestibule to the main area, went to his things, and lifted out a jar filled with money. Surely, this was far more than the land was worth. Feeling proud of the deal he had made, he handed the jar to his father.

The family's eyes open widely as they see the jar filled with money. Someone gasped.

"Who gave you this money?" Issa again demanded.

"I don't know, dad."

Issa grabbed Chijioke by the throat while Suma tried to wedge herself between the men.

"Stop," Suma cried, "You're hurting him."

The girls started to cry. These tears, more than Suma's intervention, helped Issa regain his composure. Suma put her hand on Issa's shoulder and pulled him away from her son.

Sensing a possible shift toward more understanding, Chijioke pointed a finger at Issa.

"Here we are working very hard in the hot sun, and we could be making a lot of money!"

"We were making money," Issa retorted. "How do you think I was supporting the family and you kids going to school during this drought?"

"So-o-o you knew about the diamonds?"

Suma tried to take in the enormity of Issa's knowledge and actions.

"Yes, but I was selling them to a reputable diamond dealer," Issa said softly.

"And what if there are more?"

Chijioke questioned like a prosecuting attorney.

"How can it matter now?" Issa asked. "The government is stealing my land!"

"Can we stop them?" Suma demanded.

"Stop the government?" Issa puzzled.

"Well, I thought you were supporting us with the work from the field."

Suma returned to her thoughts of having important information withheld from her.

Issa blinked his eyes in amazement. Did she really think that tuition and satisfying meals could all come from the field?

"The vegetables are not enough to feed us," Issa reported. "That's why I was selling the diamonds."

In his mind, the diamonds were simply another produce from the field of his ancestors for many generations.

Suma brought the conversation back to the present.

"Issa, what are we going to do now?" she asked.

"I don't know," he answered. "The will take everything from us and leave us with nothing."

Chijioke spoke as tears formed in his eyes.

"They promised they wouldn't do that."

Issa spit back, "Then they lied!"

Now the tears released, and Chijioke said, "I'm sorry, dad."

Meanwhile, Issa surveyed the loss.

"This land has been in my family for generations."

Suma took this as a possible defense strategy.

"There must be a deed?" she asked.
"There was no deed; it was on a handshake."
Abimbola gasped, "Oh, no."
Issa repeated, "Yes, Abimbola, oh no!"

CHAPTER

5

Fortunately, Chijioke's jar of money helped the Ndao family continue their regular life routine: working, eating satisfying meals, and attending school. Several months later, Abdalla was finishing his studies, ready to attend a university.

But, which one? As he had been coached, he applied to several schools, including N.Y.U. When a letter arrived, his family gathered around him to open it and read its contents. He was so nervous that he tore the envelope into a few pieces and nearly shredded the letter itself.

"What does it say?" Suma asked.

Her body moved as though she had chills.

"Read it, read it," the girls sang in chorus.

Abdalla scanned the letter looking for a crisp sentence.

"You have been accepted to N.Y.U."

He shouted this as he began to jump up and down.

Everyone hugged each other and was excited—except Chijioke.

***

The flights to Paris and then New York were long, and Abdalla was pleased to finally land at LaGuardia. Dressed in blue jeans, a blue shirt, and an old sports jacket, he looked much anyone from a university. And, for him at this moment, fitting in was an important theme. To get over the strangeness; to not be a stranger in a new land—this was what he craved.

After exiting the jet, Abdalla was thirsty. The flight attendants had been attentive enough, but did not serve any beverages for the last hour or so of the flight. Spotting a convenience stand, he wanted a bottle of water.

Behind the clerk was a rack of books. On the shelf just over her shoulder was a title that jumped out, *How to Make Films*. He flipped through the table of contents and would have purchased it, however it was arranged or whatever genres of film it covered. Seeing this book and being able to purchase it—this was a sign from God, he thought. Thank you, God.

Balancing the water bottle with an open book and his travel luggage, Abdalla stared at a page with photographs of how to set up a scene for filming. Rounding a corner while engrossed, he bumped into a man and dropped the book.

"Hey, look where you are going."

"I am very sorry, sir."

Feury Seger continued his walk, as Abdalla scooped up his book and watched him walk away.

Then Abdalla continued on his way to the baggage claim.

***

After tugging his luggage through the doorway, Abdalla surveyed his apartment. A small studio, it offered more space than he had imagined. The kitchen had an avocado theme around a small stove and refrigerator. A two-seat table with a plastic pumpkin tablecloth and coordinated chairs marked out a small eating area. Beige surrounded the single bed and study desk. He was glad that this came furnished because he brought only clothes and a few other things.

The doorway, however, had caused the most intrigue. Four locks of different types on the door? He had grown up without even a door on his hut, let alone locks. Did they signal safety inside or the level of danger out in the hallway and beyond?

That evening, he was on his knees praying, when he heard a knock at the door. As he got up, he wondered if the caller had been knocking for a while. Without thinking about locks and security, he opened the door. There stood the missionary, John, with a bag full of groceries.

"Hi, John," Abdalla exclaimed. "Come on in."

John stepped into the apartment, both hands supporting a barrel-like bag with celery and spaghetti noodles sticking out of the top. "My wife and I thought you could use a few things to get started, so we went to the grocery store."

"Thank you so much."

John looked at Abdalla's face, seeing that his enthusiasm was genuine.

"I hope you like the apartment."

"It's fine, no, wonderful. Thank you for everything."

"This is a small place, I know. But, I wanted to get this for you so that you did not have to pay a lot for rent. Rents in the city are very expensive."

"Yes, I've noticed how expensive everything is. Please, don't worry. I'll make sure that your rent money is paid on the first of each month."

"That's great," John said with more gusto in his voice, perhaps sounding he thought like Tony the Tiger. Even though John saw helping students as part of his ministry, John's salary was not so generous as to fund the monthly rents of any. He had instead sought to provide the lowest cost to each student. He reached out his hand, and Abdalla responded with his hand.

"Well, I'd better get going."

"It was good to see you again," Abdalla said, looking into John's eyes.

"And you as well. If you need anything, please don't hesitate to call us. And don't be afraid to ask."

"I won't."

John turned away to open the door, and then paused. He reached into his pocket to hand Abdalla something.

"Here is my business card. It has my contact number."

They exchanged handshakes and pleasantries once more. Abdalla shut the door and locked the four security devices. Then he lifted the celery off the top of the bag. He pulled out milk, cereal, potatoes, and other vegetables as well as cleaning supplies, paper towels, and toilet paper. What a cornucopia!

CHAPTER

6

Even with strong family support, the Ndao family could not have provided for the cost of Abdalla's school. And he knew that his family had increasingly limited, meager resources. He did not expect monetary support from his father. Before accepting the N.Y.U. offer, and even with its generous support, he had resigned himself to working at least part-time to pay for his own expenses. Fortunately, his student visa allowed him to work part-time, provided that he attend school full time and make progress toward a degree.

And work he did. He was a doorman at a local hotel. While the weather was warm, this worked well for him, offering pleasant greetings to guests as he opened the door. The red and gold uniform reminded him of his family's colors, and the bright effect made him proud.

He was also pleased that Africans in New York often selected his hotel. Even the man whom he bumped at the airport stayed there one time. Abdalla would not have recognized him, except that the man stared into his eyes and said, "Hi, again."

When colder weather came, however, Abdalla was not prepared—even with the hotel's winter uniform that included an insulated hat, a long thick coat, and protective gloves—to stand in the cold while heat was on the other side of the door. On those cold days, he missed the scorching sun. Regrettably, he submitted his resignation as soon as he had located another job.

He worked indoors at his next job as a telemarketer, selling season subscriptions to the opera. He had thought about having a job indoors before taking it. Plus, most calls would be to patrons for renewals. He reasoned that most patrons would have had a good experience and would want to sign up again. Part of his pay would be a commission on renewals. It should be easy.

When the calls were made, however, people were not home or they needed to talk with their spouse or they wanted to review the coming year's line-up. "Is *Don Giovanni* part of this season?" The question was easily answered, yet for some a truthful answer to their question proved to be a deal breaker. Some had seen a poor performance last year—and would critique that performance in detail. For others, their decision depended on the person cast in the leads. Again, the question could be answered promptly, but this often would not solicit a purchase because Abdalla surely could not promise that a favorite would perform on any particular night. The questions, callbacks, and confusion all meant that Abdalla spent too much time generating too little cash. So he needed to find another job—one with a dependable payment plan.

Bus boy at an upscale restaurant seemed like a perfect solution. It was indoors and close to his apartment, but did not depend on any direct sales. Abdalla could multiply his hours by his net hourly rate and compute his pay check. Sure, the amount of wasted food was disconcerting. Yet, what he didn't count on was the cost for chipped or broken dinnerware. He was strong enough to lift the tubs of plates, saucers, and cups. He tried to be careful in placing each one into the large dishwasher racks. He especially worked hard on laying out each place setting as required by the restaurant. Somehow the chips and charges added up and reduced his take-home pay significantly.

So what about working at a down-scale restaurant? It would have the benefits of hours times pay rate, but with Styrofoam cups, plastic-ware, and paper wrappers, it offered no breakage-fee deductions. The job that lasted the longest that first year was being a floor sweeper at McDonalds.

It meant that he needed to endure the wasted food and the occasional surly patron. One day, for example, a man dropped some French fries on the floor, but just walked away. Perhaps it was an accident. Then he turned around to eye Abdalla. And Abdalla recognized him from the airport and hotel. Yet, most days the job suited his needs perfectly.

CHAPTER

7

Nearly a year earlier, the army had picked up the obvious diamonds in the field. The pails and shovels were there, but the soldiers had hardly used them. Each had chided the others that they were dirt farmers or peanuts. In their jovial back-and-forth, they had collected little more than the obvious diamonds. This allowed Issa and Chijioke to dig around and gradually collect additional diamonds, which they held because they were too afraid of triggering a new investigation.

Now the soldiers had returned with workers. Issa peered out his doorway to watch this group and Chijioke as he worked in a far corner of the field. His light colored T-shirt stood in sharp contrast to army fatigues.

At first, Issa could hardly make out who was doing what to his field. The camouflage outfits made the foreigners seem like a hill of giant ants. Then gradually Issa could distinguish two groups: soldiers had guns, while other African workers had shovels, pick-axes, and pans to screen for diamonds or other precious resources.

The soldiers and workers stayed at the far end of Issa's field not far from Chijioke's corner. It appeared that the workers would harvest the diamond field from the far end toward the road so that the trucks and troops could easily connect with the roadway. The workers, however, took no care, but destroyed the vegetables and peanut plants wherever they worked, putting them into piles where they would die and dry out.

Issa crept from his doorway to the side near the roadway. For a long time, he was able to stay out of the way of the trucks and soldiers. As the day grew warmer, however, he could not contain himself. He picked up a squash at the edge of the field and then threw it down, talking loudly to himself.

"My field is lost to my family."

"I have nothing to pass on to my sons."

"They are taking my land. Why?"

Then he picked up another squash and threw it down to smash it open.

"Why did it have to work this way?"

"I have been faithful, so why is my field being ravished?"

Over and again, he repeated these and similar thoughts randomly while smashing the occasional squash.

Suma, when she spotted him, was concerned about her husband. She walked slowly to the edge of the field as well. Plants and produce had as little chance with the workers as with Issa, the one-man army. He was moving through his produce almost row by row. She watched Issa stager after releasing a vegetable explosion, then talking to the heavens or at the ground. Then he would kick or toss to the ground another plant.

Had he gone mad? she wondered.

Finally, Issa could contain himself no longer. He marched over to where Chijioke was working in the field, right passed the soldiers who leveled their guns and pointed them in his direction.

"This…"

Issa shouted, pointing his finger to all the soldiers and workers at the far end of the field, and then making a sweeping motion.

"All this…"

Issa shouted again, now including his own plant and produce destruction.

"This…is *your* entire fault."

"This is not my fault. Don't blame me."

Issa grabbed Chijioke by the neck, and they wrestled to the ground. Suma rushed over to break up the fight, if she could.

"Don't take this out on your son."

Suma was tearful.

"They are taking my land."

Issa made a gagging sound as Chijioke used the palm of his hand to push back Issa's face. Chijioke's fingers pressed against his father's nostrils.

"Don't you think someone would have found the diamonds at some point?" she asked. "This was going to happen eventually."

"Everything I have worked for is gone. Everything my family worked for is gone."

Chijioke had broken free from his father's grip and jumped to his feet. Issa ripped a plant out of the ground.

"These are mine. They are being stolen from us."

"But God is in control of this," Suma retorted.

"So are you saying God is letting these people steal our land?"

"God is letting this happen for a purpose."

"But Chijioke was selling my diamonds."

"So were you," Suma replied.

The government official watched Issa's bizarre behavior and his fight with his son. He signaled for several soldiers to accompany him as he walked to where Issa stood.

"I hear your crazy shouting," he said loudly to Issa.

"Yes, we are taking your land and we don't care what you think. We know we are taking your food supply—so if you are good to us, we will feed you. Your land is far richer than we thought. So we can afford it."

"This is my land."

"No, it's ours. If you were smart, which you are not, you would have gotten a deed by now."

The official now stood in front of Issa, face to face.

"What good would a deed have been? You would have just taken my land anyway."

"That's right. Well, see, you are smart after all."

The official laughed in Issa's face.

"You greedy man! I want my land back."

Turning to the soldiers, the official ordered, "Arrest him."

Immediately two guards each took one of Issa's arms. As they walked toward one of the army trucks, Issa could still see Suma.

He and Suma beckoned for each other.

"Don't take me away from my family."

Issa moaned repeatedly and slumped down, making his legs rubber. The soldiers, however, continued to hold him and move him toward one of the trucks.

"Please don't take away my husband," Suma called out, between her own sobs.

CHAPTER

8

Abdalla sat at his desk. He had finished his coursework. As usual, he was concluding his day by reading his Bible and praying. He lifted a letter from home, studied the handwriting on the outside of the envelope. Then he opened it and retrieved the letter inside. As he read it another time, it again brought tears to his eyes. When he finished the letter, he folded his hands in prayer.

"Thank you, God, for letting me come to New York to pursue film making. Thank you also for your provision for me. But Father, I miss my family terribly."

As he prayed, an image came into his mind. He is sitting in the hut with his mom, brother, and sisters. She is reading from the Bible to them, which she often did. Then she pauses, turns to look entirely at him

"Abdalla, wherever you go in life always follow the Lord. Always obey what God says. Always read your

Bible. Your Bible will give you wisdom and guidance. My Bible is old and torn, and it has given me faith and wisdom. You do the same."

Abdalla sees himself say, "I will, mother."

***

Abdalla position his dustpan on a handle against a wall in the dining area. Then he began to sweep the floor nearby, steadily moving dust and scraps toward the dustpan. At first, he did not notice the young man in an expensive suit who entered the restaurant. Yet something caught his attention, and Abdalla refocused his eyes. He could not believe that it was Chijioke. Could this be?

"Hello, brother."

Chijioke took off his sunglasses and stared directly into Abdallah's eyes.

"Chijioke, what are you doing here?"

Abdalla extended his arms and pulled Chijioke's torso toward his. They hugged each other for several moments before either released the other.

"I am making money, and I am not working in the field anymore."

"How did you get here?"

"I took some of my diamond money, hopped on a plane, and came over."

"Shouldn't you be helping in the fields with mom and dad?"

"After the government came and took over the land, dad and I kept getting into fights. Finally, I had enough. And with no crop to tend or harvest, dad doesn't really need much help."

"How long have you been here?"

"For two months."

"And you didn't call me? Where are you working? Where are you staying?"

"I'm on the upper east side. Well, Abdalla, I have to go."

Chijioke slid his sunglasses back onto his face. They hugged, and Chijioke walked back to the entrance, opened it, and walked away.

Abdalla left his broom for a moment and moved closer to the door. Through the window, he watched his brother get into a convertible with several beautiful girls in it. Without thinking, Abdalla waved to his brother, and Chijioke waved back.

How about that, Abdalla thought—Chijioke learned to drive.

***

Abdalla sat at his apartment table reviewing his schedule for the past week and planning his studies for the coming week. It was early, but he was tired after another week of classes, studies, and sweeping. Because he worked the weekend shift, Friday afternoon was his time off, his time to unwind from the long week—and hopefully rewind for the next week.

He looked at his watch—it was Noon—when his phone rang. Because the phone hung on the wall, he needed to get up from his chair, walk over, and answer it. This took a few rings.

"Hello," Abdalla said finally.

"Abdalla?" queried the caller.

"Chijioke, is that you?"

"Yeah. Hey what are you doing today?"

"Studying for an exam on Monday."

"How about a study break?"

"What do you have in mind?"

"Since my brother is at N.Y.U. working to get into the entertainment business, I thought that I would take him to a Broadway play."

"What do you have in mind?"

"I'm taking you to see the play, Godspell."

"I've heard it is getting good reviews."

"It opened in '71, and has been a success ever since."

"Everyone who has seen it, loves it," Abdalla said.

"It has a different spin on it. I think you will like it."

"What time does it start?"

"We'll go for a matinee, but I thought we could meet for some coffee first. I would like to spend time with my big brother."

"This sounds great. Thanks."

"Can you be ready in an hour?"

"Yes. I just took a shower a little while ago."

"Dress in a suit because we are going to this nice restaurant afterward for an early dinner."

Abdalla paused. He thought about his cash situation, and he knew more than a little about nice restaurants in New York. He wanted to go, but this was rather sudden. "Chijioke, my funds are a little tight this week. I cannot afford it."

"It's my treat."

"I'm not sure what you are doing for work, and I don't think I want to know."

"It's all about who you know and being with the right people."

"I suppose that's true," Abdalla said, but he wondered about it. Pastor John, the missionary, had been helpful to get him into N.Y.U. and make living arrangements. Even thinking about all the others who had helped, Abdalla felt as though he were an oxen shouldering a mighty harness and pulling a loaded wagon.

"Be ready and I will come and pick you up in an hour."

"I'll be ready."

Abdalla hung up the phone. Then he jumped up and down because he was so excited. Yes! I'm going to see Godspell, he thought.

***

The intercom made its excited buzzing rattle. Abdalla, in his suit, was standing in front of the mirror adjusting his tie. He stepped lightly next to the apartment entrance where the intercom functioned to approve and admit persons to his apartment. It seldom was used as nobody came to Abdalla's apartment nor did he receive many delivered meals—pizza, Chinese, or ribs.

"Who is it?"

"It's Chijioke. Are you ready?"

"Yes. I'll be right down."

Abdalla picked up his keys and wallet, and walked to the door. He walked down the stairs to the ground floor and out the entrance. Chijioke was leaning against a cab.

"Good evening, Abdalla."

"Good evening—or is it afternoon?"

Chijioke looked at his watch. "Yeah," he replied, "it's still afternoon."

Chijioke opened the back door of the cab, and Abdalla slide into the backseat. Then Chijioke slid in. After he gave the address, he engaged his brother in a conversation.

"So, Abdalla, how is school going?"

"I don't think I have studied so hard in all my life."

"You told me you are doing well. Correct?"

"Yes. That's correct. I'm really studying hard."

"Excellent. Who knows, Abdalla, you might be the next great director in Hollywood."

"Wouldn't that be something, Lord willing."

"Yeah, Lord willing. Hey, we are here."

The cab pulled up to the corner; Abdalla exited, and Chijioke paused to slap down money on the driver's hand.

The theatre area was busy with people standing in line talking as they waited to enter and with others passing by. When it was their turn to enter, Chijioke put his arm on Abdalla's back. As they found their seats, Abdalla was impressed by how good a view the seats afforded. "Thanks," he said to his brother.

"No problem."

***

After the show, the brothers took a cab to a restaurant. Abdalla knew how expensive this restaurant must be. Not the white tablecloths or wine in buckets, but the well-dressed clientele was the clue. Why even the bus boy wore a black bowtie, something he had not had to do during his days at the elegant restaurant.

After ordering, they finally had time to discuss the play in a more serious way.

"I really liked the part where Jesus tells the company of followers that no one can be devoted to two masters," Abdulla said. "They especially cannot serve God and money."

Abdalla had in mind his own financial struggles and how easy money (or its lack) could overtake his focus. After he said it, he hoped that Chijioke would not take it as a jab about his apparent wealth.

His brother, however, took it another way.

"And I especially liked what followed your favorite part. Do you remember one of the followers told the story of a man who spent his entire life accumulating things, only to die before he could enjoy any of them?" Chijioke asked. "I do not want to be like that man, never enjoying things. I want to take joy from things now."

"Perhaps the story that could capture us both is the Parable of the Prodigal Son. You have left with your inheritance in diamonds."

"True, but you are unlike the older brother in that story."

"Oh, how so?"

"Well, the older brother has to stay on the farm and labor with the father. But you left the farm first, whereas *I*, the younger brother, had to stay with the father and work in the hot sun."

"So, perhaps, you, younger brother, are suggesting that you are really the faithful one?"

"I simply know this: If you went home, older brother, you would receive the fatted calf and the bigger party. Whereas if I went home, I would be handed a hoe or a shovel so that I could do more work."

A long pause followed, covered by a waiter serving their main dishes. Sometimes, it seemed to Abdalla, conversation can be too insightful, too truthful. When conversation resumed, it was again more superficial.

"Thanks once more for everything today. What a great day we are having!" Abdalla said.

"By the way, I want to ask you, how old is your suit?"

"This used to be dad's old suit. It's a little worn, but still quite useful."

"Yeah, I can tell. You need to get a new suit."

"Brother, I cannot afford a new suit. I went to the 'hand me down' store, but I could not find anything in my size and style."

"'Hand me down'? Oh no, not for my brother. I want you to see my tailor. I'll buy you a new suit."

"Chijioke, where are you getting the money for all of this?"

"Honestly, I was hired by this one man, Feury Seger, and he has me do odd jobs at this club. I'm usually the one who checks IDs. I told him about the diamonds I found in Africa. I gave him many of the diamonds. So he put me on his payroll."

"How many diamonds do you have?"

"I had four whole jars full."

Abdalla's jaw dropped in disbelief as Chijioke, not seeming to notice, continued.

"I brought them to the United States and sold them. I made a boat load of money."

"Exactly how much money did you make?"

Abdalla asked slowly in hushed tones, not wanting to draw any attention to this conversation.

"Let's just say, I have money in the bank, an apartment on the upper east side, and a convertible."

Abdalla laughed to cover his surprise.

"I hope that you saved most of it."

"I invested it for now. I am thinking of hiring a firm to helping me diversify my investments to make them more secure while still making more money."

They both laughed together as Chijioke continued.

"Hey, have you heard from the family back home?"

"Not in a while," Abdalla said. "Not in a while."

CHAPTER

9

Suma stared at the cement walls of the jail lobby. Everything was painted a dull, light green. It's so dead, she thought. Then she saw the reason: no grasses, no plants, no pictures, nothing but this dull green. Even the army fatigue-green worn by the soldiers made the walls seem moldy, sickly.

The girls sat with her, but they were quiet. Perhaps, she thought, they were also affected by the lifeless pall hanging over this place.

When her turn finally arrived, Suma was summoned to a desk with a guard behind it. "It's all there," Suma said. "The money is all there."

The guard took the money, weighed it in his hand without counting, and called to another guard.

"Go release Issa Ndao."

The other guard left to fetch Issa, but when Suma turned around to be seated again, she saw that her chair was already taken, filled by another mother or wife for someone else. So, she stood there awaiting Issa's release.

The only person who seemed happy was guard on his way to get Issa. He stood under a bright light bulb as he waited for the security door to be opened. His liveliness might have surprised anyone walking back and forth with him. His job was to bring prisoners in and take them out. In, and out. And for this he made a good living. He owned the hundred or so feet of prison aisle and the doors to each cell. Other men might have found this work dreary, but not this one. Other men might have resorted to violence to quell the calls from the cells for release or water or less light in the aisle. But not this guard; he treated each call-out as a tribute to him and his office. This aisle gave him respect.

His biggest joy was in assigning new arrivals to cells that already housed one arrestee. And because each man stayed only a few hours or a few days at the most, he had plenty of opportunities to hone his craft. He assessed men like a social worker might, sizing them up as to potential whining through the cell bars—he put the whiner men at the end of the aisle where their cries sounded softer at his station. For men who appeared to pose threats from fighting, he put them together in one cell, just as he grouped the citizens who had merely disobeyed orders together. If one brute knocked a tooth out of another, well so be it. Yet sometimes citizens had connections, so best to let them be wary of each other. A balance of power in each cell box made for less trouble now and later.

The first door clanged open, and he stepped through to a second door. The guard at this spot slowly unlocked the door, let him through, and locked the door behind him. Each door's opening and closing sent a metal clang down the corridor of the cell-lined aisle.

The guard strode down the aisle peering into one or another cell as he passed by. His walk would be brief because, in his filing system, Issa Ndao—not a whiner, not a bully—would be near the front, closer to the guards' station and lobby.

Although Issa was not aware of the care that had been taken in assigning him to this cell with this prisoner, he was grateful for his cellmate. That man had also been arrested after his land was taken. That man also had farmed his land for generations. That man did not have a deed, did not see the need for a deed—until it was too late. Yet that man had struck a soldier with his hoe and had been nearly shot by another soldier. So that man was there before Issa arrived and would be there in the cell long after Issa was sent home.

The guard approached Issa's cell, pointed to him, and said, "You there. Issa, come with me."

"Me?" Issa asked in disbelief.

He knew the voice, but with the bright lights behind him, could not see the man's face or features.

"Yes, you. Come now."

Issa got up from his bunk and walked down the aisle toward the entrance-exit. When he was ushered into the lobby area, he saw Suma standing with the girls, who were crying because they were scared. Their heads were bowed, and their hands folded, as if they were praying. Issa could not tell. When they saw Issa, they all rushed to hug him. Suma and Issa kissed briefly. The family exited out the front door.

The guard at the desk said to the guard who fetched Issa, "They are so stupid. We give them money for food because we took their land. He gets angry so we arrest him, and they use their food money to get him out of jail. This means we get the money back."

The guards laughed, stupid civilians, indeed.

***

As Issa stepped slowly out of the lobby, through the prison entrance, and down the steps, he felt the cooler air. Breathing deeply helped him feel alive again. The dusk of the day shot colors into the sky. Although no one had mistreated him, exchanging an open field for a closed box, exchanging freedom for the drab sameness of the cell—this was too much. He would save that great exchange for death. He longed now to go home and wash this ugly experience from his skin and his memory.

As Issa stood on the step staring into the sunset, Suma tried to rush Issa and the girls back to the hut. Once home, she would feel safer, she thought, and would put this whole episode behind her. Carrying such a large pile of cash to the prison had made her feel vulnerable to some thief or crazy person. She tried to stuff a portion of the pile into each of her pockets, but this made them look unnatural. She tried to put the pile into a scarf, which she would put on her head and then over her shoulder. So, she had been glad to get to the prison safely and hand over that wad of vulnerability.

But now, without the pile of money and without the land, she felt vulnerable to life. How would the family be fed? How would the girls continue their schooling? How would Issa and she grow old together?

After entering the hut, the girls rushed to Issa as he knelt down to hug them.

"Daddy, we were so frightened," Aba cried.

She threw her arms around her father and burrowed her face into his shoulder.

"We thought we would never see you again," Abimbola said tearfully but with some reserve.

She stood behind Issa and placed her arms on his shoulders.

"We thought we would go hungry without you," Amia whimpered, Suma thought, because the girl was hungry now.

Suma gathered a bowl and some food supplies as she interjected, "But God did provide for us."

"Suma," Issa said while looking up at her, "you have more faith than all of us put together."

And for a moment, as they ate a small meal quickly prepared, things felt better.

CHAPTER

10

As the street vendor opened one lid or another, steamy smells of hot dogs drifted into the air along with chili or sauerkraut. Chijioke and Abdalla stood in line, waiting in the afternoon for their turn to order a quick lunch—and these smells of all beef dogs, onion or relish or mustard, and all the other condiments only prolonged the wait. The day was sunny, but cooler than most in early summer. And somehow, Abdalla thought, this coolness made the steam and the hot dog aroma more noticeable. Or, maybe it was simply that he had purchased so few hot dogs this way that he anticipated the treat even more. Whatever the case, he was hungry.

Abdalla scanned the mall. Many people were rushing quickly get lunch or run an errand.

"I cannot stay too long. I have to get to the bank before it closes," he said to Chijioke.

"Oh yeah, send this to mom," Chijioke said in a hushed voice while handing Abdalla a pile of money.

Abdalla took the money, but then fished for a good place to put it. Finally, he stuffed it in his pants pocket, leaving an obvious bulge.

"So how's school going?" Chijioke continued.

"I'm taking a class on Russian literature."

"Why?" Chijioke asked as his face squeezed into a sour expression.

"To understand another culture."

"What does Russian literature have to do with making movies?"

"I want to study it to expand my knowledge of Russia," Abdalla said as though he were a man of the world.

"But Russia is communist."

"I want to visit there, someday."

"Okay. I did not know you had a groovy thing for Russia."

Then Chijioke turned to the vendor.

"Two hot dogs with ketchup."

"Russia has a wealth of culture."

"Yeah, I guess," Chijioke said, shrugging his shoulders and laughing.

"So you think this is funny?"

"Yeah. Are you going to learn Russian, too?"

"I might."

Then they both laughed as the vendor handed them their hot dogs.

***

Abdalla entered the heavy revolving door of the bank and, even though he pushed with considerable force, he was slowly admitted into a new world. Massive columns stood at either side of a cavernous space with a high ceiling perhaps 24 feet high. The white marble floor stood in contrast to the dark walnut walls.

Each time he entered, he had the same experience. On the one hand, this grandeur made him feel important, confident. On the other hand, the room was so large that he felt insignificant, like one raw peanut seed stuck into an enormous field. How could one produce enough?

He walked to the table at the center, laid out the stack of cash, and took a deposit slip and a wire-transfer form. How much money was there? he wondered. Counting slowly, it came to $3,000. That's a lot of money, but mom and dad surely deserve it, and it's better for them to get it than for Chijioke to fritter it all away. He completed the forms and walked a distance to join the line.

Abdalla had been to this bank many times, but always with the same result. Six to eight tellers were at their stations, yet the line was long. He had to shuffle forward slowly as one person at a time could be helped.

This called to his mind the black-and-white photos he had seen in his class on Russia: workers standing in line out in the street to purchase bread. He had focused on Russia's magnificent culture. Yet his brother had pointed to its socialist economic system. Did the systems feel much different for him?

"Next."

He looked up to see how far he had progressed toward a teller and how far he had yet to go. Workers in the communist system had to stand in line to purchase their bread, whose price was always set at a reasonable amount. He had to stand in line to deposit the benefits of his work. Interesting, he thought. Perhaps that would make a good subject for a documentary.

He shuffled ahead a step.

What about for Chijioke? he wondered.

The systems would definitely be different for him. While so much of Abdalla's life looked like the people and the stores in the background of the Russian photographs, Chijioke's life would fit here in this rich space—if he could muster the patience for the wait.

Finally, Abdalla walked to a teller. She examined the transactions, stamped receipts, and said, "Thank you, sir. I will make this wire transfer today."

"Thank you, very much," Abdalla replied. "This is going to Africa, to my family."

Then it dawned on him that somehow this transfer from Chijioke—in fact, his brother's entire way of life—spelled a difference in the systems.

***

Suma stood outside the bank waiting in line. When it was her turn, she stepped forward. The teller counted out a large sum of money, all in cash. Suma took the money quickly, stuffed into a scarf, rolled the scarf tightly, and tied it around her neck. Then she left without a word.

On her way home, she stopped at the field where Issa and the girls were working. Two of the girls hoed the few plants that remained in the field while Aba watered them.

"Dad!" Aba yelled.

"What is it, Aba?"

"The water has stopped. The water has stopped flowing."

Issa rushed over to Aba, then followed the hose back to its source. The well is not working. This angered him, and he again picked up plants to throw them at the well. Then he kicked the well.

Suma ran to him, and helped him and the girls go home.

CHAPTER

11

Abdalla stood in front of the Metropolitan Museum of Art waiting for Chijioke. A cab drove up, and Chijioke jumped out as soon as the cab had come to a stop. Chijioke reached back into the front passenger-side door with some cash. Then he turned and joined Abdalla.

"Hey, thanks for meeting me today. I want to view what sort of artwork I want for my apartment."

"There's a lot out in the world," Abdalla replied.

"What kind of choices do I have to pick from? I like Monet art. It's very peaceful."

"That is hard to say, as I have yet to see your apartment."

"Yeah, that's right. I have to have you up for dinner so something. I like to have parties, so maybe I will invite you to one of those."

"Well, I don't want to spend all day here," Abdalla said as he eyed his watch. "I have an exam to study for."

He avoided the subject of the exam in hopes that he could be spared Chijioke's first thoughts on it.

"No, I can't spend all day here, either. I just want to see what kind of art work there is out there," Chijioke said as he gestured out into the world.

***

Later that fall, Abdalla's work at McDonalds settled down to weekday evenings. This allowed him to take a second job. Actually it was his first job in New York City, as a doorman at the expensive hotel. He felt more adjusted to New York winters. And his red and gold uniform with black trim again reminded him of his family's colors back in Africa. Like that family, he needed more cash to sustain his meager lifestyle.

He stood like a sentry releasing persons who desired to exit the hotel and admitting people who belonged at this hotel. He was proud that he had learned how to spot those persons. As people walked passed on the sidewalk only a few, he knew, were coming to the hotel. So that was no challenge. When limousines paused at the driveway, he was almost certain that hotel patrons would soon be in need of his services. No, the challenge was to spot automobiles—and not just BMWs, Mercedes-Benzs, Jaguars, and the like—whose passengers or drivers would need assistance.

The next challenge, he thought, would be to identify the potential big tippers. His back ached from offering equal service at variable rates.

A limousine flashed its blinker and turned into the driveway. Abdalla guessed that this could be a significant tip. Through the front-seat tinted window, he saw a woman in her 40s or 50s with a hat and scarf. Almost as soon as the limo stopped, Abdalla opened the door and extended his gloved hand, palm up. The woman's reddish hat included a pheasant feather and her matching coat had fox-fur trim. Her gold broach of a hunting scene included a cluster of diamonds spaced equally around the outside, making it look like a sheriff's badge.

"Please, allow me to \assist you."

She placed her gloved hand in his, flung her hips 90-degrees toward the door, and began to step one foot unto the pavement. She said nothing to him; no pleasantries, no thank you. Abdalla quickly readjusted his tip estimate downward.

After the woman stepped out, she turned to reach back into the car. "Come, Poesy, come to mommy." A little whitish dog jumped into her arms. She cuddled the dog, giving it a kiss. Then she turned back toward the hotel entrance, taking little steps. Abdalla quickly moved ahead to open the door for her, and then returned to the limo to unload her luggage.

Luggage was definitely a factor, he concluded, but in an inverse way. As life seemed to work, the more luggage to be handled, the less generous was the tip. He got her four large bags out of the trunk, closed it, and then patted the trunk lid twice as a signal for the driver to take off. With considerable effort, Abdalla muscled each bag to the front door, where the bellhop would take over and wrestle them to her room.

Not long afterward, another limo approached. This one was a stretch limo, not that common at his hotel in New York, but it instantly bespoke money.

Abdalla could barely see into it because of the tinted glass, but he sensed that it contained several persons. The driver eased the limo into the entrance area, and Abdalla opened the door.

To his amazement, several beautiful black women stepped out, one after the other, as if they were holding hands, as if their number didn't end. Abdalla nodded to the group, not quite sure what to do. Then Feury Seger stepped out and after him—Chijioke. As the two men moved away from the limo, the women latched onto them as though each woman had an assigned place—right arm, left arm, behind stroking his neck. Then as the two groups moved away from the limo, more women emerge from the limo door and then another African-American man. Perhaps a dozen people were in that limo, Abdalla thought, and produced little in the way of tip.

He needed to focus so he latched onto the one detail he knew most.

"Chijioke?"

Chijioke turned to him, "Abdalla! Good to see you."

Then he turned to Feury, "This is my brother, Abdalla."

Feury turned to Abdalla and said, "Good to meet you."

Then he turned back to Chijioke, "I'm going inside."

"I'll be right there," Chijioke replied before turning back to Abdalla.

"What are you doing here?"

"I'm staying overnight," Chijioke replied.

Then, turning to take in the hotel, he said, "Say, this place looks great."

"It's very expensive."

"Yeah, it looks it."

"Why are you here?"

"It's business."

"What kind of business?"

"A religious man like you would not like to know."

"Are you into drugs?"

"Shhh! Don't say that too loudly."

"Chijioke, how could you?"

"No, I'm not into drugs."

"Mom and dad would disown you if they knew you were doing this."

"And who's going to tell them? They don't have to know."

"Why don't you send them some more money?"

"I don't care about them, especially dad."

"No, you don't mean that. You don't want to say that."

"You should join me at the club. Then you wouldn't have to work here and work in such a pitiful job. Just imagine—the money, girls, anything you want, you can have."

Abdalla grabbed Chijioke's arm and said, "Wait, Chijioke. What about your faith?"

"I left that in Africa, too."

"You are throwing away your life."

"And be like mom, dad, and you? Struggling to make a living?"

"At least I can sleep at night."

"So can I, and in an expensive room where I have everything I want."

The head doorman approached and turned to Chijioke. "Sir, is everything alright here? Are you being bothered?"

Abdalla released his hold on Chijioke, who brushed off his shoulders.

"Oh, I'm fine. This man is my brother. We're just catching up."

Chijioke walked to the entrance and pulled open the door for himself. Abdalla stood with his back to the door as he just kept shaking his head.

CHAPTER

12

Chijioke and Feury sat at the bar in Feury's Alley Club. Music from Kook and the Gang's *De-Lite* album had just started. Chijioke was glad that fewer smokers were in attendance tonight. Much as he sought to be a party man, the smell of smoke just made him sneeze and wheeze. He bobbed with the beat, not caring for all the words of "Breeze and Soul." Feury liked his clubs to offer entertainment and relaxation.

A woman entered the club, walked over to the bar, and seated herself. The bartender approached her and asked for her drink order. As he stepped away to get a glass of the house Chardonnay, a man who had been sitting at a table scooped up his drink and ambled toward the bar. Without asking permission, he sat next to her. She ignored him, watching the bartender pour her drink and hoping he would return quickly to rescue her. Feury had noticed the entire transition.

She heard the man seated next to her mumble something, but she was not paying attention. Not responding to his question, she turned to him in a single move, told him to move away, and then she turned back as the bartender was resting her glass of wine on a small napkin. She tried to tune into the music as the man again leaned over to ask some question. She turned away from the bar to face Feury and put her back toward the man. The man kept talking. Feury took notice.

Then the woman turned her chair the other way and faced the man completely. Feury could not hear what she said. Yet by the stiffness of her back and the look on the man's face, Feury was certain she was telling the man to shove off.

Feury knew that the woman was not a prostitute. He had associates who made discrete arrangements with a few attractive, well-dressed women. He had nothing to do with their recruitment or wardrobe. He just received a commission on their efforts. He tolerated no freelancers in his club. And up until now, the man had been doing all the work while she attempted to avoid him or get rid of him. Feury motioned to the bartender to get the bouncers.

The bartender stepped away to press the button to signal the bouncers. He tried to keep his eyes on the woman in case he needed to rush back to her defense. Mostly he knew his job was to fetch the drinks, occasionally push the button, and avoid doing any of the heavy hauling.

The man then attempted to hug the woman or maybe kiss her, the bartender couldn't quite tell. The man had his lips all puckered; he must be drunk, the bartender thought. And he should have known because he had mixed a half-dozen Coke and rums for the man. Maybe that was one too many—or too soon.

In spite of their bulk, the two bouncers moved quickly through the crowd, like two sharks cutting through a choppy sea. They grabbed the man at the bar, each by a shoulder, and skillfully lifted him off his stool and toward a hallway that, presumably, led to the back door. Without a broken glass or scuff mark, they opened the doorway and flung him toward the trash. Then they walked back in as if nothing had happened.

"Miss," Feury said after he sauntered over to where the woman sat, "I think he won't bother you anymore."

"How can I thank you?"

"Nothing at all. I'm the owner."

"Now I can have my drink in peace."

"Yes, every once in a while a man comes in and tries to pick up a young business woman such as yourself. Sometimes men are looking for a free ride."

"Not from me! Thanks."

***

Feury went back to sit again. "As I said before, Chijioke, your apartment is awesome. Wow!"

"That is my home now. Just think, only a year ago I was in Africa dreaming of coming to the U.S. and having a life here."

"I'll bet your dreams didn't include anything like this. Your life is nicer than anything you could've imagined."

"Yes. Would you like to try some red wine? We could toast my success."

"Umm..." Feury said while he weighed in his mind whether to share his drink secret with Chijioke.

"Okay. I usually have a different drink...," he winked at the bartender, "I don't think I've had a really hearty red wine in a while," he said with a smile.

"You'll love it. I go to a bakery in the Italian section, and the owner, the baker, makes his own wine. It's absolutely delicious. I thought maybe we can sell it here."

Chijioke turned to the bartender, "Please get me two wine glasses and a bottle opener?"

The bartender turned to get out two red wine glasses, and placed one in front of Feury and the other in front of Chijioke. Then he handed Chijioke his bottle opener. Chijioke opened the bottle and poured two glasses.

Feury carefully swirled the contents of his glass. Then he sniffed the bouquet of cherry, oak, citrus, and an earth smell. He took a small drink, put his head forward, and slurped by drawing air through his pursed lips, forcing the liquid up into his nasal area. Then he sloshed it over his tongue and pallet. He tipped back and let the smooth, tasty liquid slide down his throat. Yes, this was a delicious wine, fruity with a smooth finish that would encourage patrons to sip it without having a too-sweet build up. At the right price, this could be perfect.

Feury quickly ran some facts through his mind. Although New York State had liberal laws about wine sales, retail shops had to be sole proprietorships. Of course, Feury thought, he worked with a wholesaler.

He had recently been approached about buying protection. Was the mob about to make sales of their bootlegged wine a condition? Still, it was good wine. So what was the angle? Maybe just making money off sales without the liquor tax. He savored the wine's aroma in his nostrils.

The mob had wrestled the numbers racket in the 1930s from blacks in Harlem, but had seemingly given it back to them a couple of years ago.

Wait. Maybe their soldiers were black instead of Italian. He eyed Chijioke in a different way. He had heard that the mob was recruiting soldiers among blacks. Had they recruited his diamond source? Chijioke hardly seemed like the muscle-type. Whatever the truth, Chijioke may have made him some money or made him a target. He would probably find out which soon enough.

He turned to Chijioke and said, "You're right. This is great."

Chijioke laughed. "What did I tell you?"

"I can see why some people get addicted to alcohol. This is very tasty."

"And because it is in New York City, you don't have to drive home."

"Yeah, but I still need to *get* home."

This time they laughed together. Then Feury raised his glass while eyeing Chijioke.

"Well, Chijioke, I want to congratulate you on your success."

"And I want to congratulate you on doing so well in business. Feury, may your success continue."

"Yes, may success continue," he said, thinking about all the ways he and his business could get played by others.

They touched glasses and took large sips. For Feury, the fruity taste—was that a hint of oak barrel—and the smooth finish all lingered.

"Thanks for letting me be here," Chijioke said.

Feury motioned that the pair move to his usual table for viewing the singers. He and Chijioke sat in silence, drinking in the singer about to perform. Chijioke thought she was about his age and stunning. Her Afro was tight and sculpted, her cheekbones high and chiseled, her lips round and shimmering red. When the music began, her sound reminded him of Sarah Vaughan, whom he had heard in concert. Unlike Sarah, The Divine One, this woman did not play piano. No matter. She still had a rich, powerful voice with a wide vocal range. And like the rich wine he had served Feury, she had exceptional class. Feury looked over, saw Chijioke's enjoyment, and smiled. He thought he had little to worry about with this rather innocent, lazy young man.

CHAPTER

13

Sometime later, Abdalla approached the club. After a bouncer approached, Abdalla told him about his brother, Chijioke. The bouncer pointed to the table, and Abdalla walked over to greet them. It was the singer's break time so the stage was quiet; instead, the patrons were noisy. As he approached, Feury stood and put out his hand, and Abdalla grasped it in a firm handshake and then put his other hand on top of Feury's. After each saying his name to the other, Feury spoke first.

"It's nice to meet you. Are you Chijioke's older or younger brother?"

"Well," Abdalla replied with a smile, "I am Chijioke's only brother, but I am the older one."

"So, you are attending N.Y.U. and your major is film. So are you also an actor?" Feury asked.

"No, I'm studying to be a director."

"Just as good. Do you have any films out?"

"No, I am working on my first film for gradua-tion."

"You can make a lot of money in the film indus-try."

"I'm not sure how much, but I've been told one can."

"Well, I'm always looking for more ways to make money."

Feury welcomed Abdalla to the table. The three sat together, this night without the girls or the bounc-ers. The club became increasingly crowded as people continued their talking, laughing, and drinking. Abdalla sipped a single drink the entire time.

At 2:00 a.m., Abdalla looked at his watch, rose from his chair. Chijioke gave him a hug. Then Abdalla took his coat and stepped carefully toward the bathroom. When he entered, he saw men using the small shelf just above the sinks and below the mirrors to snort a substance Abdalla took to be cocaine. Sens-ing that they might not want any watchers present, he stepped into a stall.

Should I wash my hands as if everything is nor-mal? he thought. Or should I head straight for the door? When he finished in the stall, he chose the first option and washed his hands, as he thought, How to join rich people in their activities—that is a difficult task for me because they are always seeking to escape while I am seeking to connect.

***

Chijioke entertained himself not so much by going to clubs as by being a tagalong. He sought out the rich people and simply followed them into their favorite pastimes. For example, he got an invitation to attend a polo match at Meadowbrook Polo Club on Long Island. He watched how the crowd actually followed the players mounted on horses chasing a ball and striking it with their mallets. He used his feigned interest in the sport to strike up conversations with others, and he mingled with any unengaged spectators.

He learned about the finer art of wine tasting at O Bon Vin on Seventh Avenue. He used Feury's method of slurping to gain an even greater taste of the subtle elements that had gone into the grapes and vinification process. He used his real interest in wine to learn about how wines are perceived and valued.

Yet he didn't just stay with the rich. He also attended horse races at the tracks, watching those with scorecards making bets and playing the odds. Here he found it more difficult to strike up a conversation, even about the odds or which horse betters were choosing—or avoiding. They wanted to focus their attention on the sport.

From his apartment association, he met a person who invited him to that person's expensive apartment for a party. Again, Chijioke used it as an opportunity to meet people.

Through all of this, Chijioke had the sense that he had friends because he had a few connections that led him to a wider pool of contacts. They came to his parties; he saw them at other parties. He worked a few deals, like the wine with Feury, but he never really made it inside any of the circles of the rich. He had simply come closer to them than most other persons.

***

The camera room at N.Y.U. provided core training for all film directors in the program. Knowing how to work a camera was fundamental when a director asked camera operators later to achieve particular focal points or effects. Abdalla held a camera for his first time while his professor pointed to one button or twist-option after another.

This should have been energizing for Abdalla, but all he could think about was going to sleep. By the time he had got home from the club, he had had only a few hours of sleep. Words like *cinematography* sang in his ears like a lullaby. He closed his eyes for just one moment.

After a few minutes, the student next to Abdalla thought he was sleeping and shoved him a bit. Abdalla lifted his head with a start. He yawned like a lion about to take an afternoon nap. After class, Abdalla replaced the camera in his holder and headed for the door.

"Wait, Abdalla," he professor called. "I know this can be boring, but hang in there with me."

Some students nearby attempted to cover their snickers as they continued walking. Abdalla lowered his head in shame.

"I'm sorry, professor, I was up late at my brother's apartment last night."

"Save the parties for the weekends. These classes are important."

"Yes, sir."

"Abdalla, don't let your brother interfere with your studies," his professor warned.

"I won't, sir."

"You know, Abdalla, we really care about our students here. Is there something…"

"Thank you, sir. This won't happen again."

Abdalla continued his walk toward the door. His head remained lowered as he slunk out the door.

***

Already it was late morning by the time Chijioke had gotten ready to leave his apartment. He had decided to get some baked goods from his favorite Italian shop.

He approached Ramon at the counter.

"Hey, Chijioke, how are you, my friend?"

"Doing very well, thanks. And you?"

"I'm having trouble with the little woman. We had a big fight."

"Oh, well I'm sure it will all work out."

"Yes, it will. I love her and she loves me." They laugh.

""So, my friend, what can I get you today?"

"Today, I would like the Italian Easter bread."

"Yes, you like the sausage-and-cheese filling. Don't you? It can cover both breakfast and lunch," Ramon said with a smile.

CHAPTER

14

The government had now taken over about three-fourths of Issa's field. Only a small patch, the front left-hand side remained for the family. Soldiers watched not only the workers but also the family whenever Issa, Suma, or the girls worked their remaining plot. The part remaining had vegetables; most of the peanut cash-crop had been destroyed by the diamond diggers.

The money that Chijioke sent (what should have been nearly 20 years of wages!) helped maintain the family's prior life, but only for several months. The bank had used an unfavorable exchange rate in converting dollars to the local currency. Issa's diamond sales had helped the family live far about what his neighbors had suffered during the drought. Yet, the loss of the field with its crop meant that Issa needed to repay his seed, fertilizer, and equipment with much of the remaining cash.

The food bowl showed off the new situation. Whereas at one time the bowl offered rice, peanuts, and vegetables as well as chicken and fish, now it only offered rice and vegetables. And, despite the absence of the two sons in their early 20s, even the quantity of their reduced menu seemed in shorter supply.

The girls cried like a Greek chorus in some tragedy. "But mom I love school," whimpered Aba.

"So do I," agreed Abmibola as tears ran down her cheeks.

She had found a strong, supportive network of young women who had all made plans for a better future for their families and their state.

"We - can't - stop - going - to - school," Amia choked, her tears were so intense.

"Girls, we just don't have the money to send you to school any more. These last few weeks will be the end," Issa explained as he and their mother attempted to comfort their daughters.

He knew that the girls had gone to the school far longer than their meager funds permitted. Yet, he and Suma had hoped that more funds would be wired to them from America.

"But dad, I'm going to the next level of school," Aba continued.

"But girls, we don't have the money to send you," Issa repeated.

"Dad! We - love - school."

"I know, girls. But there is no way we can send you anymore."

Issa thought that, except for the pleading, the girls sounded like mourners reaching the end of their grief.

"Let's pray," Summa said, breaking the breath-filled silence. "Let ask God to provide for us."

Just as their heads were bowed, they heard a knock at the hut entrance. Issa went to the doorway to find their pastor outside. He invited the pastor to enter. Then he spotted a cloth bag the pastor was carrying. When Suma heard Issa invite the pastor, she jumped up to join the men. Each family member greeted the pastor in turn.

Then the pastor spoke, "I hope this is not an inconvenient time. My wife and I were praying this morning, and we felt the Lord tell us to bring these food items to you."

"We did not have much to eat tonight, and we were praying for something to eat," Suma replied.

"I guess that I am an answer to your prayers. God is good all the time."

"Yes, and all the time, God is good. You are indeed an answer to our prayers."

"My wife and I went through our garden and picked these vegetables. We cannot eat them all," the pastor said as he offered the bag to Suma.

"Oh, thank you, pastor," she replied as she took the offering.

"How are you and your family otherwise?" the pastor asked turning to Issa.

"I'm afraid the government has taken more of the land. We just have a small piece of land for crops. Everyone in the nearby village is gone or is preparing to leave."

"And we told the girls we cannot afford to send them to school," Suma added.

"It is hard for them. It's hard for us all," the pastor said.

"It's most difficult to part with my land," Issa agreed.

"It's the government," the pastor said. "It's difficult because the government is stealing what your family had."

"The government has stripped almost everything from us," Issa agreed. "The hard part is they stole our crops, put me in prison to steal our money, and won't help us even with food.

"The government doesn't want you or any of us to prosper. But, you have a wonderful church family that cares for you," the pastor said, trying to turn the conversation toward a more hopeful note.

Issa, however, focused on the land and his money situation. "I cannot get any more money from the diamond dealer, so I don't know how we will get money. He wants more diamonds. But, of course, with the soldiers at my field, I cannot gather any more stones."

"Maybe the diamond dealer can make a deal on your behalf with the government. How is your money situation?" the pastor asked.

"We had some money," Suma said softly, "but it was depleted when Issa was jailed."

"Well, as I say, maybe you should approach your dealer," the pastor said in an equal hush. Then he spoke up, "By the way, how is Chijioke?"

"Abdalla said in a letter that Chijioke is doing quite well for himself. He looks very good," Issa said, the twinkle coming back in his eyes as he thought about the successes of his sons.

"How curious," the pastor said. "Maybe Chijioke is looking too good."

CHAPTER

15

Chijioke's apartment was thumping with a jazz beat and a wailing saxophone. People were gathered in small groups holding drinks and chatting. He surely had a skill in bringing people together to have fun, and this party would ensure that he received more invitations to join attendees in other events.

Chijioke carried a red wine glass, welcoming or greeting guests, when he spotted a young African American woman seated by herself on a love seat. Her features were refined and her skin lighter than many women he had dated. Without knowing a thing about her, he was already in love.

"My name is Chijioke Ndao," he said to her as he approached. "What is yours?"

"My name is Tyesha Maxwell," she said without getting up. She extended her hand.

Chijioke gave her a big smile, accepted her hand, and kissed the top of it lightly. "Did you come with anyone?" he asked.

"Some of my friends told me about the party, and I came with them. Your parties are famous around here."

"Are you dating anyone right now?"

"Not until now," she said seductively.

Chijioke gave her another grin and sat beside her.

***

The next morning, Chijioke wanted to introduce Tyesha to his brother. The couple took a cab to Abdalla's apartment building. He peered up the spiraling column of stairs and sighed. Abdalla had no elevator. After climbing the stairs, Chijioke paused for a few seconds to catch his breath—and his composure.

Yes, he thought, I am now ready. He went to the door and rang the buzzer, but no one answered. "I guess he is not home," he said to Tyesha. "We'll have to come later." Holding hands, they walked down the stairs.

***

The center of the sound room was a large console with what seemed like hundreds of sliding switches as well as volume controls and on-off switches. The sound engineer who sat at this console was positioned to look through a large glass window onto the next room which housed microphones and a few musical instruments—a piano and a trap set of drums—as well as a few sound effects devices. The sound engineer needed to balance the various sounds in order to produce the most pleasing experience, while at the same time keeping unwanted noise and interference out.

Abdalla had been experimenting with the console for a long period, setting up the controls for his assignment, and practicing the switch from microphone to another. While making notes on his script, he realized that he was late. Another student came to the door and gave a polite knock. Abdalla dropped what he was doing and beckoned the student in.

"Hey, are you almost done?" the student asked, not waiting for a reply, but coming into the sound room.

"Yes, I'm all set," Abdalla replied, grabbing his books and exiting before the door had swung shut. That was a smooth transition, he thought.

Out in the hallway, students were moving from one lab to another. Others were entering and exiting the building. One student dropped into file-step with Abdalla, walking directly behind him, but Abdalla didn't notice. He pushed the button and then turned to wait for the door to open. "Jeff," he said as Jeff came to the elevator.

"Abdalla, how's it going?"

"Good, good. How are things with you?"

"Boy, school is pretty intense."

"I still cannot believe we are here."

"You're from Africa, right?"

"Yes."

"Then this must be culture shock."

The elevator opened and, after others exited, they both stepped inside.

Then Abdalla continued the conversation.

"It is hard adjusting to being away from my family, doing my schoolwork, working, studying..."

His voice trailed off as he pictured everything he was doing.

"You know, you are right, Jeff. This is pretty intense." They both start laughing.

***

That evening, Abdalla was again studying. He had already finished preparing for his exam in the morning. Now he was studying his Bible, taking notes as though it were another textbook for his career, for his life. He had read the story about Lazarus (who died and went to heaven) and the rich man (who died and went to hell). The rich man begged to have Lazarus bring just a drop of water. The rich man begged that Lazarus be raised from the dead in order to warn the man's other rich brothers. This called to mind the song "Learn Your Lesson Well" that he and Chijioke had experienced at *Godspell* and hummed afterward.

With his devotions finished, Abdalla closed his Bible, bowed his head, and prayed, "Father, thank you so much for bringing me here to N.Y.U. Help me remember all that I have studied for my test tomorrow. And please watch over my rich brother, Chijioke. Amen."

Just then, his buzzer rang. Someone was at the door downstairs. Abdalla went to the intercom and asked, "Who is it, and what are you doing here?"

"It's Chijioke. I just wanted to see if you wanted to go with us to get something to eat."

Abdalla looked at his watch. "It's already 12:30 a.m., Chijioke. It's very late. I have an exam tomorrow."

"Oh, the night is young. Come with us, brother."

There was a pause. Abdalla was planning his next objection when his brother continued.

"Come on. I want you to meet my new girlfriend."

"Why don't you come up."

Abdalla said this with a deep sigh he hoped hadn't been heard. He pushed the lock-release button so that his brother could enter. Then he went back to his desk to close his books and notebooks, putting things in a neat, orderly pile.

A knock sounded at the door. Abdalla walked over to open it. As the door swung open, he saw Tyesha standing before him with Chijioke behind her.

"This is my girlfriend, Tyesha," Chijioke said.

Abdalla saw the same beauty that had attracted his brother to her. Realizing that he had hesitated too long, he thrust his hand out.

"It's nice to meet you," he said.

"It's nice to meet you as well," she said.

"Well, brother, come with us now," Chijioke insisted.

"No. Thanks for the invitation. It's very thoughtful to include me. But I have an exam, and I am very tired."

Seeing that Abdalla would not change his mind, Chijioke took Tyesha's hand, and they turned around and began to walk away.

"Chijioke," Abdalla called out.

Chijioke turned around again.

"Chijioke, how are you doing?"

"I'm doing really well. I have everything I need."

He looked into Tyesha's eyes.

"Right, baby?"

Her lips mouthed the word right in response.

"Have a good night."

Abdalla said this as though it were a blessing at the end of worship.

"You too," his brother replied.

Then Abdalla shut the door so that he could rest.

CHAPTER

16

Not far from Abdalla's apartment was the New York venue of an exclusive china shop headquartered in London. It sponsored its own polo team—so several of Chijioke's new polo contacts had recommended it—and it had served British royalty for generations. Whatever the cost, Chijioke thought, this would be the place to make his purchase.

Even though he was well-dressed as usual, he found the sales woman to be a bit off-putting. "Are you here to make a purchase?" she asked. He thought to himself, What other purpose would I have? Yet, he said nothing. Instead he stepped to the display of sets and began viewing them. Finally, he said, "I'm looking for some china to use for my parties."

"And what sort of parties do you have?"

"I entertain my friends a lot, and I also entertain some business associates."

"Well," she said, introducing a warmer tone in her expression, "let me help you find something exquisite."

Chijioke had sensed something. He hadn't been treated as poor or a potential shoplifter. No, it was something else. It was as though he were not old money, not part of a lineage of money, not eligible for aristocracy.

Then he wondered whether the sales woman might have been friendlier had Tyesha been with him. No, he understood that the sales woman, even in her servant role, felt superior to him and his new found wealth. It was like one laborer telling another to mind his place in the social order. He concluded that she would have treated him in the same way, however he had approached her, and he walked out of the store without another word.

***

Abdalla sat in the classroom with about 25 other students. One part of the exam was to write a story in screen-play fashion. All the techniques were at his finger tips ready to hold pen and display them. But he stopped—and stared at the blue book with lined paper. What story? Had his studies up until now been fruitless? He whispered to himself, "Father, I need some help to write a story. I just cannot think of anything."

He closed his eyes. He saw the color green and the smell of the peanut plants: red vinegar, sweet at first and then delivering a pungent tang like an onion. He tasted their scent on his tongue that was fresh and then slightly bitter. He remembered the day that he raced his brother to the field, how his brother had tricked him, but how he still won the race. He felt the sweat from running so hard on that sultry day. He remembered his father coming to the field and how his father would spot him taking quick breaks to stretch his muscles from the long hours of back-breaking work.

Suddenly Abdalla sat up in his chair. He checked his watch. Good, he had only been entranced for a few minutes. "Yes, I can write about that," he whispered to himself. "Thank you, Father."

***

Chijioke was still on Madison Avenue. He brooded about his experience at the china shop. He spotted an exclusive men's store. This time he walked slowly by, looking at its displays. He turned around and paused. He peered into the display window a second time. He smiled. "I have to have that," he whispered to himself. He walked into the store as other people were coming out.

***

Abdalla had walked South and West, past the public library, to The Drama Bookstore in the Theatre District. He took a small elevator to its floor and then stepped into the shop. It was surprisingly small, he thought. He wandered through the store, sampling one title on display and then another. He lifted each book up, inspected its cover, and read the description on the back. He opened each book to read its table of contents. Still he could not find exactly what he was looking for.

Then he spotted a worker who was carrying a stack of books. "Can you tell me where I can find books on directing movies?" he asked.

The worker put down the books at a nearby desk and led Abdalla to the sections marked directing and making films. "I'm Frank," the worker said. "Are you directing a project?"

"Yes, I'm a student at N.Y.U., and I am doing a film project."

"N.Y.U.? That's great," Frank replied with enthusiasm.

"Yes, God did a miracle to get me here."

"You sound like you have an accent. Where are you from?"

"I am originally from Africa, and I will be here for a few years to complete my degree."

"Well, welcome. Do you plan to stay here? To become a citizen?"

"Right now, I am concentrating on my studies. After school is over, I can explore becoming a citizen."

"Well, if you're becoming a film maker, you're not going to want to go back, I'll bet. Especially if you make a name for yourself with successful films."

"Lord willing."

"I have talked to others about this. They also came to our store because they wanted to be successful in this business. Of course, some just want to keep updated in the field. It gives them an edge."

"I suppose as in any industry, one would want to keep skills up to date and understand the trends."

"Exactly," Frank said. "The more you do that, the more you will become more valuable than the next guy. I wish you every success... Say, what is your name?"

"I'm Abdalla Ndao. And when I need to upgrade my skills, I will come to see you. I mean, if you are still here, Frank."

"Yeah, just ask for Frank Simon. I'll still be here." They shook hands. "So what's your script about?"

"My script is about my experiences here in America, mostly good. But I do not have it down on paper, yet."

"Then you may want to get a few books on screenwriting."

Frank took Abdalla to the shelf and lifted up *Screenplay: The Foundations of Screenwriting* by Syd Field.

"We have sold a lot of these."

Then he handed Abdalla another title and another. Then the phone rang.

"Hey, I have to get this call. Good luck with everything, Abdalla."

Abdalla wanted to return the greeting, but Frank had rushed off. Abdalla inspected one book and then another, deciding to get the three books that Frank had selected. When it appeared that Frank would be on the phone for a while, Abdalla waved a good-bye and headed for the cash register.

***

The spring afternoon was warm and fresh as trees were budding and the grass was a vivid green. Dandelions had bloomed, scattered their parachute balls of seeds. Apparently this cycle had already taken place once before because green foliage was spawning new yellow flowers. Chijioke found a few of these first-bloom dandelions and picked them for Tyesha. She admired them as he went for ice cream.

When he returned, she gently launched the blossoms from her lap onto the lawn in order to receive her cone. The ice cream was already soft and dripping down the side of the edible container. Both licked the sweet gooey liquid in order to keep from dripping while enjoying every drop. Then as they reshaped the top of their cones with their tongues, they saw one another in awkward grimaces, and began laughing.

How delicious, Chijioke thought, when he saw that Tyesha had ice cream all around her mouth. He leaned over to kiss her lips and mop up the white ring of ice cream. Once she caught on to what he was up to, she reached over, pulled his head into hers with her free hand by placing it behind his neck, and then she planted one slurp kiss after another on his lips and mouth area.

Everyone who walked past them could not avoid seeing their behavior or know that these two were in love. The laughing, the playing with ice cream, the open kisses—all these signaled a deeper bond. Had Chijioke found something deeper than money and its benefits?

***

The late spring air had lifted Abdalla along his return route to his apartment. He could not wait to open his books and learn more about screenwriting. When he entered his room, he put his books down on the desk, sat in his study chair, and surveyed his apartment. What a gift it all was. He lowered his head in thankfulness. Then he swung down on his knees next to his desk because he was so overcome by gratitude—and regret.

"Father, I hope I don't ever have to go to work in the fields again. I love my family and give you every thanks for the blessing they are to me. But I had to work hard to scratch a living there. My father still works there, and he must now work harder for his sons are gone. I love this opportunity in the entertainment business you have given me. Could this also be my family's future? Could you also grant to my family what you have given me so far? And I pray that my dream of becoming a movie director fits your plan for my life. Amen."

CHAPTER

17

Issa sat on the cold floor in the jail cell. Two small cots were available for seating, but Issa preferred this place. He needed to cool down; spending time in jail was not helping him provide for his family. He recognized this. Yet, somehow watching the government take away his family land, turning good soil upside down to sift for diamonds, watching everything he had been taught by his father and his father's father before and all the ancestors—that was too much.

His failure to maintain connection with the ancestors—that weighed most on him. The Christian notion of the communion of saints had been important to each of his forbearers. Many generations ago—he was not quite certain how many—his ancestor had plotted out that piece of land, had nurtured native crops on it. Later, ancestors had begun raising different crops. The changes were gradual, and each generation passed on its knowledge and wisdom to the next generation.

Now Issa knew that he stood as a failure on all counts: the government had taken the land; the soldiers had destroyed the crops on it; and both his sons were gone not only from Casamance, but even from Africa. Among the ancestors, he was to be pitied. He might as well die in this cell because he could not be buried with the bones of his ancestors.

The guard who managed detainees in the cells came over to Issa's cell.

"Issa Ndao."

The man's voice, even he kept it low, had a booming quality.

"Yes, that is I."

The guard opened the door and motioned for Issa to walk out.

"You are free to go."

"I'm being set free?"

"Yes, and I encourage you not to get into another fight with the government officials again. Do you hear me?"

"I do, but they are taking my livelihood. I am a farmer. I cannot feed my family with such a small plot of land. My land has been in my family for generations."

"I don't care about your puny problems."

Issa walked out the door and walked ahead of the guard toward the exit doors. When the first set of cell doors was closed, Issa moved forward to peer into the lobby. He looked around for Suma, but did not see her. He turned to the guard behind him.

"Is my wife here?"

"No."

"Who set me free?"

"The judge threw out the case. If I were you, I would keep my mouth shut. The judge did you a favor. But if you continue to give the government officials a hard time, then it won't look good in front of the judge next time."

The guard then stared directly into Issa eyes.

"He will keep you in jail for a *long* time. And I would rather not have to take care of you."

"How am I supposed to feed my family?"

"That's not my problem. But having you back would be my problem. And I don't like problems...get it?"

Issa got it. The good treatment from the past two visits was over. Next time he would not be treated as a landowner, but as a criminal or at least a civil mischief-maker who needed to be taught a lesson. He had cooled down. Now the deeper message was being heard. As he walked into the cool night's air, he realized that he wasn't wanted at his farm, and he wasn't wanted in this jail, and he would not rest well among the ancestors. Where was he wanted?

***

As Issa walked toward home, he hoped that his arrival would be a good surprise for Suma and the girls. Then he thought about how they would find sufficient food. As he was working on these things, he approached the part of the village where huts had been abandoned. He did not spot the old man roaming among them. The old man, however, spotted Issa, bent down to avoid being seen, and quickly moved toward the road. As Issa strolled by thinking about other matters, the old man suddenly sprang from behind some foliage into the road, and scared Issa.

Before Issa could do anything, the old man cried out, as if talking to persons in the empty huts.

"There he is, the religious one!"

The old man made the word religious sound mocking or even funny. He continued to taunt.

"Just got out of jail?"

"Old man, how do you know that I got out of jail?"

Issa had stopped walking and now he headed toward the old man.

"I know everything."

"You do?"

"I also know that you will be leaving here and moving somewhere else."

"If you know so much, then where will I move to?"

"The United States."

"What? You are a crazy old man. Such a move is impossible."

Having dismissed the old man as deranged, Issa pushed the old man aside and proceeded on his walk home. Issa wished, however, that such a move were possible so that he could see his two sons again.

***

Suma and the girls were in the hut, praying their evening prayers. They asked God for Issa's safe return. Issa paused to hear this and then walked into the hut. Upon seeing him, the girls screamed with delight as Suma rushed to give him a hug.

"How good that you are here. What happened?" Suma asked.

"The guard said that the judge threw out the case."

"That is exactly what we prayed."

Aba nodded her head.

"Yes, father. That is what we prayed."

"But the guard warned me if this happens again, the judge will not look favorably on me."

Abimbola said, "The Lord got you out, daddy."

"Yeah, the Lord."

Abimbola frowned. Issa had spoken with such a sarcastic tone.

And Issa felt bitter as though Abimbola had attributed this good turn of events to some old technique, like the ancient ritual of using cow's blood to remove suffering from a hut or family. It seemed so easy to Issa that God was thanked for the good turns of events, but never implicated for the suffering. Why did he sometimes feel more like the cow than like the redeemed hut?

"Yes, Issa, it was the Lord," Suma said firmly. "God got you out."

"Well, who put me in the jail? Why did I have to go there in the first place? Why is this happening to me and my family? We have done nothing but follow the Lord."

"Girls, please go into the other room while I talk with your father."

Sensing the tension, the girls quickly moved to their sleeping area in the other room.

"Issa, I don't know why this is happening to our family, but we have to believe there is a purpose."

"A purpose?" Issa said with disdain. "I don't believe that."

"There is a purpose in our suffering," Suma repeated. "God is providing for us." She said each word with emphasis.

"No, this is not strengthening my faith. Have the girls been able to go to school? No. We have no money to buy anything, not even food. Why don't we have the money? Because the government stole the land that has been in my family. I grew crops on that land."

"I know you are angry. But there is a reason for all of this."

"For the past couple of weeks that I was in jail, how did you eat?

"We picked some produce, and the people in the village helped us with food."

"Well, I'm glad to hear that."

"Also, Abdalla has been sending us money. It's true, we don't have the money for the girls to go to school. But, we have enough to eat. God is providing for our daily bread. Everyday God provides for us to eat."

"What if God doesn't supply our daily bread?"

"Then God isn't the Almighty. Are we only to trust in God when times are good? Do we think we cannot trust God in the bad times? Especially in the bad times? God can be trusted at all times. I don't know when or how. But God is our heavenly Father."

"I'm afraid that God won't provide for us in the days ahead. I feel so responsible for providing for our family. Yet, I feel so empty for ways to achieve this. I'm afraid we're at the cliff's edge."

Then Suma and Issa hugged each other in a mixture of confidence and fear.

***

The roof on the church seemed to rattle as standing worshipers swayed with the music, singing as loudly as possible. Suma and the girls were again near the front singing and lifting their arms.

Then the pastor called for a hush, as the congregation moved to another song. The singers brought the jubilant praise down to a whisper as they began singing a hymn the missionaries had taught them:

"Jesus, I live to you, the loveliest and best..."

Suma recognized that this song echoed what she had said to Issa, but she needed to sit down. She was hungry, and all the singing had taken her energy. Then the second verse began:

"Jesus, I die to you, whenever death shall come..."

At this, Suma began to cry. Her daughters next to her saw this, and Amia also had tears streaming down her cheeks.

"Momma, I'm hungry," Amia said to Suma.

Then Abimbola joined in, saying, "So am I."

And Aba said, "So am I, mom."

Suma then gathered them all into her arms, and agreed, "So am I girls."

And they hugged one another as the song finished.

After worship, Suma and the girls joined the line to talk to the pastor. A woman who worked at the church approached the group.

"Suma, we missed Issa today."

"He is very discouraged. He believes God has abandoned him and us."

"After all he's been through, that's probably a pretty natural response."

"Do you think so?"

"We will ask the church to pray for him. Not everyone shares your strong faith, Suma."

"I'm afraid that today when we are all hungry, even my faith is not so strong."

The woman lightly grasped Suma's elbow as if to help lift her up out of a chair.

"I think we have a solution to your food needs."

"What is it?"

"My son is a manager of a food distributor in the city. He wanted you to have the food in the truck outside."

At this, the woman, Suma, and the girls stepped out of the line to greet the pastor, and all circled around to get to the truck. In the back were bags of rice, couscous, peanuts. Crates were filled with an abundance of various plants, and all different kinds of vegetables and fruit in cans. Then Suma spotted a large fish wrapped in clean, but well-used sacks.

Without a word, the girls stepped up on the truck's bumper, reached for a handful of roasted peanuts, and ate them still in the shells. Suma thought to stop them, then realized how hungry they must be and how satisfying, at least for a moment, the fibrous husks might be.

"I hope this helps," the woman said. "The Lord put it on my heart to give this to you."

Suma could only mumble, "Thanks so much," as she also took some peanuts.

"We need to help one another and see each other through."

After swallowing, Suma, hugged the woman and said, "Please tell you son, thanks. We really appreciate his kindness. We are truly hungry."

"Have you eaten anything today?"

"No... not yet."

"By the way, you will need this."

The woman presented Suma with a can opener.

"Yes, we will need that, it appears. May God bless you and your son, abundantly."

The girls got up into the back of the truck, and each took a ripe banana. Aba gave one to her mother, who then walked to the truck's passenger-side seat and climbed in. The woman got into the driver's side, started the engine, put it into first gear, and started the brief journey to the Ndao hut.

***

The hut's floor was clamy as the sun was high overhead shining down on his former field, now empty of workers or soldiers or government officials. As Issa knelt on the packed dirt, he could only hear the sound of a slight breeze that blew now and again through the window openings. He was glad that this day was Sunday, a day of rest for him and his family.

Issa was in the position for prayer, but he waited for an attitude of prayer. His heart was heavy with grief at all he had said to his beloved Suma, and how he had behaved in front of his girls. His stomach made a gurgling sound; he was hungry. To him, this sound and feeling were like a prayer gong, calling worshipers into prayerful action. Words welled up from someplace deep inside him. These were not his hungry words, angry words, or shameful words. These were simply the overflowing of his heart:

"Father, in heaven, I know you are able to do all things. I have been so angry at what has happened to my family, our ancestral land, and me. It seems so unfair. Only now do I see it was also unfair when I had the diamonds and could sell them a few at a time. I had much, but did not want to share with others in the village or through the church. And now all I see around me is hunger and pain.

He fell silent, waiting for more words to well up.

"These men who have stolen my land make me angry. It's the only food supply for my family, and we are hungry."

He paused as he took in a larger view of the field.

"But maybe I have behaved as though it was mine alone. Could I have treated you as though I was now the owner, and not you?

He paused again.

"I want a faith like my wife's faith. I want to be more as I was when I was a younger man. I want to trust you. Please, God, help me, help us. Please make me to be a good example for my family."

"I believe in you, but please help my unbelief, Father. Amen."

His lips continued to move, but Issa was not aware of what he was praying anymore. He was just aware of such a divine presence as though a heat or bright light were combing through his body and mind and spirit.

The sound of a truck stopping and doors slamming brought him back to where he was, kneeling on a cool floor.

Oh, no, he thought. The government officials are back to fool with me. He listened carefully, hoping to pick up a clue as to the reason for this visit.

But wait...was that Suma's voice? Now Issa was confused.

"These bags are so heavy," Suma said.

She led a small parade as she and her daughters entered the hut.

"Watch out, girls, so nothing falls or is wasted."

Aba came running to her father.

"Daddy, daddy, look what we have."

In case, Issa didn't see or grasp the full scene, Aba continued in a shrill, happy voice.

"Food!"

Amia carried her bag over to him to see.

Issa got up and headed to the door. A woman was struggling with a large bag of rice. He bent down to grab the slipping sack and ease it to a safe place. Then he walked outside toward the truck and was overwhelmed by the variety and quantity of food; the truck was full.

Suma was reaching into the back to get another basket when Issa approached her from behind, scooped her into his arms, and hugged her. He whispered into her ear.

"Thank you for your faith. You are such an encouragement to me. I love you so much."

Suma smiled at him, and then she kissed him.

CHAPTER

18

Every restaurant or club needs a face-lift from time to time. Feury Seger had schedule his club's redo in August when the city was hot and many of his clientele took vacations. To increase revenues and to accommodate a new partnership by sharing some floor space, Feury knew that his New York City nightclub was to be divided into two parts. He didn't want to watch the transition, however, and turned the design and construction headaches over to his new tenants.

Now as he opened the door and peered inside, he was pleased with what they had done with his part. Most people would still know this public, retail side. He relaxed a bit. Whether single, a couple, or in a group, they could still come to get great food and drinks at typical prices—and in a nice place. He turned to view the reviews carefully framed and mounted to the right. Just right.

At the root of Feury's success was what he called his "splash technique." The chef, for example, had won his share of *New York City Magazine* honorary mentions; placing any higher would have been too expensive. The competition and getting the club's name in the reviews—that was enough because it would splash the club's name in the right venues. All Feury had wanted was restaurant reviews with solid endorsements. Getting lots of kudos would take regular ads or other promotion.

He imagined guests at the tables and servers rushing with drink and food orders. The servers were all in their late 20s or early 30s, well dressed and well groomed, attentive but never intrusive. He trained each one as to how he wanted them to serve. Then he viewed the raised stage and pictured singers and jazz performers engrossed in their must. The stage seemed high enough to allow most tables to view the performers. He stepped to a small sound-and-light control board near his table. He inspected the room again. The fixtures were first class as were the sound and light systems.

Now he looked back toward the entrance. The room now seemed nearly square. This made the room appear to be a ball diamond shape (the entrance was like home plate). Patrons entered at one corner of the building (with the restrooms near the entrance-exit). The restaurant kitchen and wait staff all functioned out of the left side of the building (the door to the kitchen was behind third base). The stage was in the back corner somewhat between the dining and bar areas (running from third to second base). On the right side was an expansive bar with other, higher bar tables and stools (running from first to second base).

Clearly someone paid attention to all the details without always spending the most. The room reflected his values; the club would provide each patron with what he or she was seeking in fine dining and entertainment.

That segued to Feury's new cash machine. Behind the bar (at about first base) ran a hallway that went back behind the entire diamond. Feury had vowed to himself that he would never go back there. Even now that he was alone, he would simply stay on his side. He leased out that floor space on a monthly basis with a commission or bonus system. If the club had any illicit or illegal activities for which patrons paid far above the usual rates, it would be here. Of course, Feury didn't know about them.

Yet, Feury admired this lessee. It could identify a need among a specific cultural group and build a service to supply that need. In many respects, the lessee operated the same as any other business—except for the nature of the goods and services provided.

At one time, Feury dealt only with other African Americans. He preferred it that way because if he really needed to deal with such criminal elements, then he would have preferred to benefit the African Americans who had provided these services and him a steady fee.

Yet the trust among African American criminals was more personally rooted. This meant that relationships extended only within a small circle, and Feury had no access to any of these circles. In contrast, the Italian Americans had a more international, professional approach that made the circle wider on the front end and the punishments harsher on the backend for those who didn't follow the rules.

Rules. That word made Feury smile. He thought of an acquaintance, Roberto Woods, who tried to set up a discotheque and had been shown around by "an associate." When Woods rejected five locations, the associate had beaten Woods nearly to death and demanded $3,000 to let him live. Later when Woods had set up his disco on his own, he didn't phone the associate for "assistance." The associate returned with 15 others to trash the place. The associate then told Woods that this was the sort of thing the associate could "help to prevent." Later, Woods' bullet-riddled body was discovered in Queens.

Feury's rule was simple: "Go along to get along." That was a much better business practice. He paid for 6 doormen, but only 3 or 4 ever came to work. As a private club, he could allow patrons to stay past closing time of 4 a.m. when patrons "brought their own bottles." Such bottles were available at a stand near the bar beginning at 3:30 a.m. It often led, however, to tensions or even brawls.

For that reason, Feury never stayed at the club past 2 a.m. This way, he was not as personally implicated. He made good money while he slept. Another good business practice.

This infiltration of his club was like a cancer slowly spreading through a healthy body. Gradually more scum clogged the arteries, more corruption crippled the liver, and more losers reduced the lung capacity—until finally the patient was dead. Feury knew the day was coming for his club. And good business practices would schedule him for a profitable departure into retirement in this world.

***

Later that evening, the dining area was filled with enough patrons to keep the wait staff and table cleaners comfortably busy. The jazz singer was in the spotlight and the band was really a DJ off to the side. The cigarette smoke made the ceiling a hazy blue.

The bar area, in contrast, was filled with business men dressed in suites and narrow ties. A few women were each talking with a man at one or another of the bar tables: little black dresses with lots of cleavage showing; extravagant laughs at whatever he is saying; encouragement to have another drink and buy her one as well. It all seemed provocative, but relatively harmless.

A person could easily move from this bar area to the hallway behind the bar. An unattached woman, sporting an Afro and dressed as though she were going to a jazz concert, carefully slipped around the bar and headed down the hallway. She followed a couple; the woman ahead opened a door, took the man's hand, and drew him inside. She walked past that door, then peered into a peephole on another door, where she saw people snorting cocaine and getting high.

She hurried past other rooms until she arrived at the last, largest room at the back. She peered through the door's peephole and saw a group of men at a table playing poker, a group of bouncers milling about in a kitchen area, and an associate at another table with a lot of cash, a money counter, and a calculating machine.

There, seated at the poker table, was someone who looked like Chijioke from the back. She noted that every chair was filled with what she took to be other high rollers. An associate was at the counting

table instead of watching the entrance from the hallway. She paused to think things through.

"So how much is here?" the associate asked the
counter.

"About seventy grand."

"That's all?"

"Whad'ya means, 'That's all'?"

"That's not enough."

"Maybe they just wasn't buying this week."

"Well, then next week has to be better."

Tyesha peer again and saw that a guard was not
present. She turned the door knob and snuck in. She
remained quiet approaching the bouncers in the
kitchen area until she is standing next to some man.

"Excuse me," she said rather innocently, "I'm
looking for Chijioke Ndao?"

Coffee cups hit the table. The associate yelled out,
"Who is this woman and how did she get in this room?"

Chijioke turned around to confirm the voice he
heard. "On, no," he said.

"Do you know her?" The associate shouted in disbelief.

"Yeah."

"Well, get her out of here!" the associate barked.
To the other he said sternly, "Who let her back here?"

"Don't worry, I'll take care of things," Chijioke
reassured. He got up and walked quickly to her. "Hey
baby. What are you doing here?" he asked as noncha-
lantly as he could. Then he took a quick glance back
in the associate's direction.

The associate motioned for him to get her out of
the room, while Tyesha continued to look around, her
mouth hanging open at what she thought she saw.

Chijioke grabbed her nearer arm, lifted her up a bit, and started driving her toward the door. This action wiped the confusion from her mind as she shrugged off his man-handling attempts. They both paused as he let her go.

She asked sweetly, "Why haven't you called me?"

"I've been b-u-s-y."

"Take it outside," the associate directed.

Chijioke started once again to push or pull Tyesha the other way, out the back door into the alley. But she refused to be pushed around or even move.

"I've called several times," Tyesha continued in a little girl innocence as if she were either drunk or in shock at where she was.

"Look, I've been really busy. Why are you here?"

"And I knew you would be here. But I checked on the other side and couldn't find you, 'Jokey, so I followed a couple down the hallway, hoping to find you."

"Baby, you cannot see me at the club anymore."

"I have something very important to tell you."

"Can't it wait for another day? I've got things to do. I've got a big stake in this game. If you don't leave quickly, I'll lose it."

"No, it can't wait."

Chijioke was more than frustrated at her presence—and at his absence from the table. He had been running behind and now he could get dialed out of the game without a chance to win back his stake. He grabbed Tyesha's elbow as if to strong-arm her down the hallway and out the door. He needed to impress the associate and the men at the table.

Chijioke yelled, "What is so important that you have to come to the club to bother me?"

"Why are you yelling at me?" Tyesha said in hurt, confused voice.

It sounded to Chijioke as though she were about to cry.

"Get lost, whore!" Chijioke shouted.

By this time the bouncers were next to Chijioke to help him.

"You said you loved me. Do you remember?"

"I would never say, 'I love you,' to you."

Chijioke pushed her to the wall.

"But you did."

Chijioke turned to the bouncers and hissed:

"Get rid of her!"

"You said you loved me and would take care of me."

"Baby—I-I can't talk right now."

"But this is important."

She said placing all her emphasis on her final word.

"*Not now,*" he retorted.

The bouncers then moved quickly from Chijioke's side to grab her, each taking her by an arm and forcing her out the door into an alley.

"Chijioke!" she called over her shoulder. "I'm pregnant! Please help me!"

"Not on your life," he called back.

"You'll pay for this," she warned.

"Get lost, slut!"

The associate had now come to Chijioke's side. "What's that all about?"

"The girl claims I got her pregnant."

FAITHFUL BROTHERS?

"Hey, I don't want any trouble around here. *Do you understand, mister?*"

Then the associate pushed Chijioke up against the wall.

"I have a very lucrative business here, and I don't want any trouble. This is how I make my money."

Again, the associate pushed Chijioke's head up against a wall so hard the bouncers who watched thought they would hear a crack. Then the associate released him and walked away.

Chijioke attempted to straighten his fine suite, but he had been embarrassed in front of everyone. Well, it was only money that would be lost tonight at the table, Chijioke said to himself, as he straightened his tie and lapels, and walked out the door to the hallway. A man had to stay loose and flexible to make it in this town.

CHAPTER

19

Abdalla had cranked some erasable onion-skin paper into his typewriter. He had a pencil eraser tucked behind his right ear. Books were propped open on his desk. He was re-reading what he had written so far, not sure if he needed to use the eraser or just keep plodding ahead.

The intercom buzzed, and Abdalla got up to answer it. "Who is it?"

"It's me, Tyesha, your brother's girlfriend. I need to talk with you."

"Come on up, then," Abdalla said, flicking off the intercom and pressing the front-door lock release button. He didn't need this interruption, but maybe it would be brief. He looked around and decided to close his books and straighten his desk a bit before she arrived.

When he heard a knock and opened the door, Tyesha stood there visibly upset. Her hair, although in a tight Afro, was messed up as if something sticky had matted it in a few places. Her cheeks were tear-stained. Her eye shadow was smeared.

"Come in, please."

"Hi, Abdalla."

She slowly entered his apartment, carrying a small bag.

"I hope I'm not bothering you."

"What is the problem?"

"I need your help. As you know, I have been dating your brother for about six months."

"No, I didn't know that. But perhaps it's been that long since we met."

"Well, I'm pregnant. When I told my parents, they wanted me to give the baby up for adoption. But, I want to keep my baby. So my parents kicked me out."

"How unfortunate for you. I am very sad to hear this."

"Yes, and I went to the club where Chijioke hangs out, and I told him about the baby, and he treated me terribly—and had me thrown out."

Her lips trembled as she seemed about to cry.

"Now… Now, I have nowhere else to go."

And a fresh wave of tears cascaded down her cheeks.

"Hmm. My friend who got me here to the U.S. is a pastor. Maybe he can help you find somewhere to go."

"I—I just don't know what else to do."

"I'll call my pastor to see if he can help you for tonight."

"I just need a place to sleep. It's too cold out to sleep on the street, and I have nowhere else to go. I have a change of clothes with me. And I wouldn't need much space."

"Your parents kicked you out on a very cold night."

"They are ashamed of me."

"They should be ashamed of what they did to you."

"Well, it's really all my fault. I have been hanging around with a group that parties every night. My life seemed so boring. I wanted to get out. That is how I met your brother. My momma always told me that the Lord would have to work hard to get my attention, and now God really has it."

"Tyesha, I am not proud of what is happening with my brother. Do your parents have faith?"

"My parents are very religious. I had a close relation with God before I met these people I've been hanging out with."

"You are speaking to a brother in the Lord. I hope we can become good friends, but to be honest with you, I don't feel comfortable having you stay here with me. So I will phone my pastor; he will know what to do."

"Really? That's good to know. I think I've come to the right place. And I understand about not staying here. I don't want to put you out."

"So you are probably hungry. And you are in luck because I already went shopping." Abdalla went to his refrigerator and gathered a carton of chocolate milk and two pre-made sandwiches—chicken salad, one of Abdalla's favorites. He placed these on his table. Then he retrieved two glasses and two plates and placed them on his table. He poured the milk into each glass, carefully, as though he were metering out a specific number of ounces in each cup.

"This is good," he concluded.

"I haven't eaten all day. Abdalla, this looks very good."

"When we are done, we will pray."

CHAPTER

20

The diner was a real step down from Feury's restaurant, but its bright, overhead lighting at each table helped Chijioke stay awake as he read his *New York Times* and sipped a continuous coffee. Long ago, he had finished his steak and fries, and sometime more recently eaten a piece of pie. The lack of cigarette smoke, he thought, also made this a good spot to spend some time. Now and again, he would inspect his watch. Finally, when he had had enough coffee, cream, and news—and when it was late enough—he called for his check.

The waitress brought his bill, $10.45, and he reached into his pocket for change. As he arrived at the cash register, she said, "Ten dollars and forty-five cents."

He had more than enough money to pay the bill. He handed her a $20, and she began reaching into the trays to get the correct change. Chijioke, however, had already started to head toward the door.

"Keep the change, sweetheart," he said over his shoulder.

"Thank you, sir," she called back, quickly pocketing nearly a half-shift's base pay.

"I've got to get some sleep," he said as he exited.

***

Abdalla exited McDonalds, gathered his coat and cash from his paycheck. He usually waited until daylight to pick up his check and then cash it through his employer because he felt safer walking home. He had never got comfortable using a bank, in part because his finances were so close to zero. And, using cash helped him in his tight budgeting process. Tomorrow was the first of the month, and his rent was due. To keep his commitments, he needed to cash it tonight because tomorrow his rent was due. Tonight he had second thoughts about whether such diligence was wise or even worthwhile. He had thought about asking Pastor John for a day's extension. He had considered taking a cab home just to be safe, but this would cost him nearly a day's wages, money he could not spare to give to a cabbie.

He was tired, and he ambled a little slower than usual. The moon was completely hidden by clouds, and he stepped from one light post to the next. Then sounds behind him brought his mind into focus. It sounded as though two men were directly behind him. He walked faster; they walked faster.

Then Abdalla turned around quickly in hopes of surprising them and seeing their faces. At this pause, they took advantage of his stop to grab him and throw him to the ground. Quickly they felt through all his pockets. The cash from his paycheck—gone. His wallet—gone. A single kick to the ribs, and they ran away, leaving Abdalla on the ground.

When Abdalla got back up, he felt his pockets again, and said in a hushed tone, "They took my money. How am I going to pay for my rent? Dear God, why did this have to happen? And now? All my money is gone. What am I going to do? I have no money to get home. I'll have to walk back all the way home. I knew not taking a cab was a bad idea."

Across the street, the man walking looked a lot like Chijioke. Wait, that really is him, Abdalla thought.

He called out, "Chijioke! Chijioke!"

Then Abdalla crossed the street in hopes of catching up to him.

But Chijioke got nervous and began walking faster, not recognizing his brother's voice.

Then Abdalla called out, "Chijioke, it's me, Abdalla!"

And Chijioke slowly turned around as if he were about to wrestle with a ghost.

"Abdalla, what are you doing on the street so late?"

"After work, I cashed my paycheck before the restaurant closed. Then, I was walking home when I got mugged. My rent is due tomorrow!"

"How much do you need? Maybe I could help you."

"They took all of my money."

"That's awful."

"I don't even have enough to get to my apartment."

'I'll get you there."

"Maybe a few dollars to get a subway."

"Here, let me get you a cab."

"Oh, my, thanks. How have you been doing lately?" Abdalla asked.

"Okay, man."

"Where are you going?"

"Nowhere. I'm just walking around."

"Why don't you stay with me?"

"Okay, at least for tonight."

They both turned and moved toward the street and yelled in unison, "Taxi!"

***

The brothers pursued their different lives in New York City. Chijioke continued to have lots of money in his pockets—and lots of women on his arm. He would take one attractive woman to an expensive restaurant one evening. Have a different woman to his apartment on the second evening. Go to a movie or theatre production with a third woman. Play the sensitive man by walking with a fourth woman to window shop and take in the sites. Take a fifth woman to a disco for a night of dancing. And these dates were on the weekdays.

In contrast, Abdalla continued his work behind the counter at McDonald, getting orders ready for customers. He would stay after class to practice setting up the camera equipment—even though it often fell on the floor. He would try again, but the same result. He knew the reason for this: he had operated many hoes, but he had not worked with mechanical things while growing up. He had little sense of buttons, releases, thumbscrews, and the like.

He worked with other students to review filmscripts. He studied with others in the student lounge in order to keep up with all his classes. And he would try the camera equipment one more time—but the same result. Frustrated, he again put it back on the shelf.

***

Chijioke had helped Abdalla with cab fare, and Abdalla had helped him get away from his apartment for a week. As the two brothers sat in Abdalla's apartment, it was clear to Abdalla at least that he needed assistance. The calculator was old, but it recorded results in black and red. And by the end of the month, everything looked red to Abdalla.

"Chijioke, I need money for rent and school. I have nothing left."

"Do you want me to help you?"

"Yes. I don't want to bother you, but you said that if ever I needed help to ask you. So I'm asking you."

"What do you need help with?"

Why is my brother torturing me? Abdalla thought to himself. Why does he make me ask him in detail, when he knows that my paycheck and wallet cash were stolen? Settle down. Just tell him.

"I need money for my schooling. Because my paycheck was stolen, I used my school money to pay the rent. Now I'm short for school."

There, he thought, was Chijioke happy now?

"Relax. I'll help you. Don't worry."

"Thank God you are here," Abdalla said more gracefully. "You are such a faithful brother in a crisis."

"No problem."

The telephone rang, and Abdalla got up from his chair at the desk to answer it.

"Hi, John. … Yes, I would love to go. … Okay, Thanks."

Abdalla hung up the receiver and turned to his brother.

"You will never guess what just happened. I got a job for the summer, working on a movie set!"

"That's really cool," Chijioke said, dryly.

CHAPTER

21

The upstate New York Finger Lakes were known for their beauty. By standing on a hillside at Keuka Lake, one could see the lush green foliage of the trees as the hill ran down to a wide river-like series of lakes. By sitting in a boat and looking up the hillsides, one could see angled woods run up to wooded plateaus. The moisture in the air made the distance bluish and gave depth to the scene as each hill or plateau was a lighter shade of blue.

The movie location was situated between these two angles, positioned right at where the hill and lake met. The movie set was marked by a long-legged folding chair with the word *director* on the black back support. Next to that was a similar chair, but without any marking. There Abdalla sat with the script in his lap while the film crew moved every which way to set up the cameras, lighting, and sound equipment for the next shot.

Out of the crowd of technicians emerged the director who climbed up into his chair, put his elbow on the support, and buried his face into his hand to get a quick break from all the commotion.

After a short time, the director lifted his head, looked at Abdalla, and asked, "So, do you like the script?"

"Yes, very much."

"John told me you are going to N.Y.U. I hope that you've been studying hard."

"Yes, for the past couple of years, I've studied very hard."

"And I hear you're at the top of your class? What year are you?"

"Now that I am a junior, I am at the top."

Abdalla spoke wistfully as he pondered what that might mean. Beating his brother in a foot race was one thing, but winning a four-year academic climb up a mountain meant what? He focused back on the conversation.

"I've heard a lot of good things about you, you know. I hear you are very successful at school."

"My success in school comes from the Lord."

"Well, in that sense, all of our successes come from God. Anyway, I'm glad to be working with you," the director said as Abdalla nodded in agreement. "Now, how do you think we should frame this scene?"

Abdalla and the director talked further about the action and the backdrop. They got up from their chairs and moved to various spots in order to frame each shot and isolate the still camera shots from those that needed to move to get a greater sense of drama. What about shadows? How could the sound be picked up best from this stance? Abdalla wrote some notes in his script.

Soon the morning with its hectic activities was changed into the Noontime. The buffet for all the workers reminded Abdalla of a feast, in spite of the simple nature of the foods themselves. Spread out were various breads as well as a variety of meats, cheeses, and greens. The condiments were the widest assortment he had seen in some time. Then potato salad, mixed greens, mushrooms, green pepper slices, carrots julienne, and sunflower seeds. Baked beans? He thought that he would have some. Finally, dessert was small squares of chocolate cake with a choice of juices or coffee.

As Abdalla sat at picnic tables with the crew, he looked away from the buffet. He thought of his work at McDonalds. The food at McDonalds was surprisingly good, he thought, but the focus was on serving the customer within 2 minutes of walking in the door—not on setting an exquisite table. Then he looked back at the buffet. How things are served can be as important as what is being served. The script provided the what; but as a director, he needed to provide the how. As the shooting of this movie was drawing to a close, Abdalla counted this as an important insight.

***

The next morning Abdalla was again by the director's side. The pair needed to finish filming even as they closed their work relationship. The crew milled about setting up the next scene.

"I hope as your director, Abdalla, that you have learned some skills to be successful in this business. I've observed how faithful you are to the writer's script and the human interaction that unfolds as actors work together in their roles. You will do very well in this business. Just keep working hard, and it will continue to pay off for you."

"I will do that. This job has been such a good change from my occasional hotel doorman duties and especially sweeping floors at McDonalds."

"Oh, I doubt that you will have to do that anymore."

Just then, a crew member signaled that he needed to talk with the director.

"Okay," he said, "we are ready to start."

Abdalla and the director got up from their chairs and walked to where the scene was being shot. The director patiently shared with the crew and the actors what the scene was, what the action among the characters would be, how their bodies should be position, what hazards might be encountered—"watch out for this," Abdalla would remember. It impressed Abdalla how much the director made a team out of a group of persons who knew little about each other. The actors were set. A small chalkboard and clapper was snapped—so that picture and sound could later be synchronized later—the director said, "Okay, roll 'em," and filming the final shot took place.

***

The newspapers—*The New York Times* and *The Wall Street Journal*—had been laid on the breakfast room, connected to the kitchen by a butler's pantry. Seated in the center was a white china breakfast set. Just off the right-hand side was a coffee cup with eight crisp sides on a saucer that looked like a miniature plate. The coffee server also showed this angularity, as did the bread plate, if the white cloth napkin has been removed. In fact, the only thing that looked out of place was a tall, crystal-clear juice glass filled with orange juice.

Chijioke sat at the table smearing marmalade onto his toast while reading a front-page story. He was so engrossed that he did not hear his part-time cook and housekeeper enter.

"Anything interesting in the paper, today?" she asked.

"Nah. Just the same old mergers and political corruption," he replied. After he read further, he exclaimed, "This thing is really big!"

She sighed in a matter-of-fact way, "They usually are, sir. They usually are."

***

The filming was now finished, and the only thing that remained was to pack up all the gear and put it back into its storage place. A lot of it had been rented, so this needed to be packed and registered as returned. Other gear was owned by and came with the professional who worked it. This needed to be packed and taken by its owner-operator. Then there were the construction boxes for miles of electrical cords, small lights with clamping mechanisms, parts to make the railroad-like tracks for the camera stand.

And hammers, wrenches, clamps of every sort, other tools—and even things for which Abdalla could not imagine their usage. The place looked like the floor at McDonalds after parents with younger children had attempted to have a family meal. Scraps of junk everywhere.

A bond of friendship had built between the director and Abdalla. They had said their good-byes in one form or another several times already. But this had to be the last time, Abdalla thought.

"Thanks, again, for all your help this summer, Abdalla. And tell your pastor thanks for recommending you," the director said.

"I will thank him as well for such a fine opportunity this summer. I have learned so much. Like, how much work is needed to film a single scene."

"We threw a lot of information and odd-jobs you way. Don't let that deter you from pursuing your dream, Abdalla. Every dream takes effort and sacrifice. Some days you will want to quit, but 'hang in there baby'," the director said, quoting a commercial cum bumper sticker.

This struck Abdalla as odd; the director always strove toward original expression. They shook hands.

"If you ever need a letter of recommendation, please let me know. And, Abdalla, I want to give you this before you go. I hope this will help you with your expenses."

As they shook hands, the director handed Abdalla an envelope, which Abdalla accepted without hesitation.

"Thank you so much," he replied.

With that, Abdalla turned and walked away. With his back to the director, he carefully opened the envelope and looked inside. His eyes bulged wider. The amount on the check was the biggest amount he had ever received for working.

"Thank you, Father," he prayed.

CHAPTER

22

The Sunday truckload of vegetables and staples from the church to the Ndao family had lasted quite a while. Suma had smoked the fish and included small pieces with some of the meals so that it would last longer. Now little was left. Suma, Issa, and the girls sat on the floor eating dinner. Their bowl had only a few vegetables, the last pieces of fish, and a handful of roasted peanuts.

Outside the night was clear and quiet. Then the stillness was interrupted by a knock at the hut opening. Issa got up, went to the opening, and peered out. He saw his neighbor with family and belongings only partly visible in the darkness.

"What are you doing?" Issa asked his neighbor. "Where are you going? Wait. Are you leaving?"

"Yes, my friend. I am taking my family away from here. We are going to go to a new village. We cannot stay here; we are struggling to find enough food."

"So are we."

"My children go to bed at night and cry. My wife was beaten and almost raped yesterday by one of the guards—in front of my children!" the neighbor said in disgust.

His wife stepped forward to reassure him. Issa saw that the skin around her eye was swollen with a slight cut. When she realized that her attacker's marks were visible, she stepped back and hung her head in shame. By this time, Suma had also come to the opening to see what was taking Issa so long.

"I-I-I'm so sorry," was all that Issa could mumble.

"It is not safe for my family to be here anymore. I am taking my family to another village that is much safer, especially for my precious wife."

"No, I can see that. I certainly don't blame you. We also have considered moving."

"Well, I hope to see you again, maybe in another village."

As the neighbor said this, Issa stepped outside and gave the neighbor a hug. Suma also stepped outside had hugged the neighbor's wife. They wished one another that God be with them, and the neighbors walked to the trail.

***

Soon the family returned to finish its meal, and the girls began cleaning the area. Issa sat on the floor, and Suma joined him. They began a whisper conversation.

"What happened to her?" Suma whispered.

"He said that his wife was beaten and *almost raped* by one of the guards yesterday, *in front of the children*," Issa hissed.

150

"In front of the children?"

"Yes. He doesn't feel safe here in the village anymore."

"I don't blame him; I don't feel safe, either." Suma thought a moment. "Where are they going?"

"They don't really know."

Then Issa hesitated wondering whether he could ask the question on his mind.

"Has anything like this happened to you or the girls?"

"No, thank God."

"I think it will be important to stay together in the field."

Issa rubbed his head with his hand and then took Suma's hand into his.

"I don't know how much more I can take. This is really making me angry."

"I don't feel safe being here."

"I'm surprised to hear you say that. Then we should leave to."

"Where will we go?"

"I don't know," Issa said.

Again he paused to consider his next statement.

"I am too afraid to leave you here with the girls by yourselves."

"I would feel safer for the girls if they were in school, but I know that this is out of the question."

Now Suma hesitated.

"Should we talk to the girls about this?"

"No, I don't want to scare them." He paused. "I would kill any man who touched you or the girls."

And Suma believed that he would.

***

Because the growing season was ending, the sun having baked everything nearly dry, the field was dusty and the plants, thirsty. The girls worked in the field, now that they did not attend school and that their older brothers had left home.

Abimbola saw that some of the vegetables needed watering, so she gathered up the buckets, took them to the pump at the field's edge, and began pumping. Nothing came of it. The pump creaked as though it were working, the handle felt heavy as though the pump were drawing up some cool water, Abimbola worked the pump quickly just like she had seen her father and brothers do many times. But no water came.

Sydney, a younger guard about Abimbola's age, watched Abimbola carry the buckets over to the pump, work the pump, and get frustrated. He had chewed on a dried grass reed all morning, thinking about her; maybe it was time to do something. His job was easy enough, just watch for anyone attempting to disrupt the mineral extraction. Yet his helmet was little protection from the sun's heat. He needed a distraction. So he took the reed out of his mouth and threw it over his right shoulder. Slowly he walked straight toward her, keeping his eyes on her the entire time.

At first, Abimbola didn't notice him. She was too frustrated with the pump that took her energy, but repaid her with belches of air instead of dollops of water. Then she noticed him coming straight toward her from his guard position. Maybe he wanted a drink of water, she thought. Ha! Let him get it for himself. She wasn't going to give aid to her oppressor.

Then she thought that she couldn't anyway because she couldn't get the pump to work. This brought a smile to her lips so that when she turned to check on the guard, she thought that she may have looked too friendly, too inviting, and too much a willing villager. She bent back down trying to appear as though her attention was actually on something else.

She watched as the shadow of this man—or boy, really—darkened the dirt where she was staring and fussing.

"Can I help you with the pump?"

"I-I-I guess so. I can't get it to pump much, though."

"Well, it looks like you haven't got it to pump anything but air," he replied rather smartly.

Then he offered real help.

"You see, you were pumping fast enough, maybe even too fast, but you weren't going deep enough. You've got to lift the pump handle all the way up so that the pump mechanism goes into the well water to actually get some."

His explanation all seemed good enough to Abimbola. Perhaps he really was here to help her.

"Let me show you. You hold a bucket under the spigot, and I'll do some pumping."

She positioned a bucket and, as he pumped, the faucet first gurgled and then spew water into the bucket, one whoosh of water after another, just like she had seen when a neighbor had milked a cow. In just a few pumps, that bucket was full. So Abimbola got another lined up and another and another. Soon all the buckets were full—perhaps too full. She could not lift one bucket with both hands on the handle, both arms attempting to lift.

He picked up one bucket with one hand, using his other hand to gently tip the bucket and top off other buckets, while reducing the water level in this first bucket. He handed it to her, and she found it surprisingly lighter. She carried that one, while he picked up two buckets. This is going unexpectedly well, she thought.

"What's your name?" he asked.

"Abimbola, and your name?"

"Sydney," he said with a slight British accent. "My parents used to live in Australia, but then we moved here when I was small."

"Well, it's nice to meet you. Are you in the military?"

"Yes. Do you work in the field all day?"

"Well, until I can go back to school."

"School? You? You go to school?"

"We used to go to school. My parents don't have the money to send us anymore."

"So, do you know how to read English?"

"Yes, the missionaries taught us."

"I have a letter from my grandparents in Australia. I want to read it, but I can't," he murmured. Then he said in the hushed tone of embarrassment, "I don't know how to read or write English."

"Well, I can help you with that. Bring me your letter, and I will read it with you."

"Gee, thanks! Well, I'd better go before the other guards get suspicious."

He lowered his buckets to the ground, quickly but without a spill. Abimbola put her bucket down as well, slopping a little even though she thought she was much more careful than Sydney had been.

"Thanks for help me," she called to him as he followed his track back to his post.

"No problem. I'll see you later," he called back over his shoulder.

"Yes," Abimbola said as she smiled. Later, she said to herself.

Just then Sydney turned around and waved to her.

"I'll bring the letters with me next time."

Issa was disappointed with this. He was working in the field, but he was too far away to hear what was being said. And once he had looked up and caught the scene he was too far away to protect her. Some peanut plants had received rather harsh treatment as the young soldier approached his daughter. Yet as far as he could tell, the interaction was innocent enough. He needed to stay closer to his girls and wife in order to keep them safe.

CHAPTER

23

That evening, Issa heard a knock at the hut entrance. When he reached the passage, he saw a young man dressed in casual clothes. Yet, they seemed dressy. Issa judged him to be about the same height and proportion as the young man in the fields earlier. Issa took him to be a nice enough young man, strong and sincere. The young man's shirt was simple and white. And he could be wearing slacks instead of blue jeans. If this were indeed the same young man, then his sentiments lay with the occupiers, not with the village residents.

As Issa inspected him, he also heard activity in the field. His listening had led to an awkward silence in the doorway.

"I would like to speak to Abimbola, please," the young man said while looking into Issa's eyes.

"Who are you?" Issa finally asked.

"My name is Sydney. I met your daughter today when I helped her with water buckets."

While he was speaking, Abimbola arrived at the doorway, suspecting that Sydney might not wait until he was back in uniform—and in front of his peers.

To Sydney, Issa said, "Yes, I was watching you."

He turned to Abimbola and said, "You may go, but stay close to our home."

Abimbola walked outside and steered Sydney to some rocks for sitting near the fire pit and not far from the doorway. After they were seated, Sydney handed her several envelopes.

"These are some of the letters my grandparents have sent to me."

"I can read them for you. Where do you live?"

"I live in the orphanage near the city."

"I have heard that they are very cruel there."

"Yes, they are. My parents would never have approved."

"Where are your parents?"

"They were killed in a car accident in the city. In their will, I was supposed to go back to Australia to live with my grandparents. My parents even provided money for my trip and care. But the government stole those funds and took me to the orphanage instead."

He paused for a moment and Abimbola let the silence sink in.

"I get up every morning and put on the uniform of a government that has robbed me."

"My father is also angry about how he has been robbed of our field. I think I also understand."

Another pause.

"Well, let me read these letters and tell you their contents. This letter begins with your grandparents telling you how much they miss you."

"I miss them as much. They came to get me out of the country a few months ago. But as you can see, they were not successful."

Abimbola read another letter.

"Your grandfather had a stroke. I guess I'm not sure what that is."

"It's a lack of blood to the brain."

"That sounds serious."

"It is. My father was a doctor. One of the women who run the orphanage always complains that she will have a stroke if our chores are not done."

They laughed and talked for a while. Sydney had been sent to school for a while, but he had not paid attention enough to learn to read or write. Then his parents died, and schooling was no longer a possibility.

Abimbola read letters lifting out important details. Sydney put the details in the context of his life. A wonderful friendship was forming. They looked into each other's eyes, but Abimbola turned away shy and embarrassed. Then Sydney gently put his hands on her jaw and guided her lips to his for a kiss.

Issa had happened to wander near the entrance at just that time and accidentally witnessed his daughter's first kiss. He was now staring and unsure whether to be angry or pleased for her.

Abimbola caught her father's presence out of the corner of her eye. She quickly broke off the kiss, picked up paper and pen, and acted as though she continued to write a letter back to the grandparents.

Meanwhile, Suma had watched Issa watching them, and she took her husband's ear to pull him away from the doorway.

"Issa, you come away from that doorway."

"I just want to make sure that my daughter is safe."

"Listen, you met Sydney, and he seems like a nice young man."

"Yes, he *seems* nice enough—but he *works for* the government."

"Well, he isn't one of them."

Just then, the older couple heard a short scream outside and scuffling. They rushed to the doorway with Aba and Amia. At the doorway, they saw Sydney in handcuffs. One of the guards had Abimbola in a tight grip, and this had caused her to scream as she trashed about trying to get away. Another guard was reading a portion of the letter that Abimbola had just written back to the grandparents.

"So, Sydney," the government official snarled, "you think you can escape from the orphanage? You can't get away from me now!"

"How did you even know that I was here?" Sydney protested.

"We have been following you for the past few days. The orphanage was getting very suspicious each night that you might take off."

Issa had been drawn outside because of the way the guard was treating Abimbola.

"Don't you dare hit my daughter," he threatened.

Meanwhile, Abimbola wrestled with the guard in order to get to the government official.

"Where are you taking him?" she demanded.

"Someplace we call Hell where he can rot for eternity," the official sneered.

This confused Issa.

"He's a good boy. Why don't you just leave him alone?"

Suma hit Issa in the back in the hope of keeping her husband quiet—and out of jail for once.

"And who is speaking on your behalf?" the official asked.

Then he leaned into Issa's face and sneered, "You're an old man. Pitiful, really. But I don't take pity, I take action."

"Leave my family alone," Issa said in a forceful manner as he spoke each word.

"And what if I don't leave them alone? What are *you* going to do about it?" the official queried as he struck Issa's breastbone to emphasize each word.

The official used his chest to push aside Issa as the official rushed toward Sydney.

"Boy, you have lost my patience. I'm not sure what I want to do with you."

The official and Sydney were nearly nose to nose.

Then the official backed away and began to pace. He stopped to eye each family member; when they saw his attention, they stopped struggling with the guards.

Sydney also noticed the shift in attention.

"Please don't involve them. They have nothing to do with this."

"I've had enough, boy. You are a poor excuse for a military guard. You are of no use to me now. You ran away for the last time."

Then Abimbola took up Sydney's cause as if to acknowledge his self-less plea. "Please leave him alone."

The official then drew a pistol and shoved it into her face.

Abimbola screamed in fright at the man's response to her plea. Issa reacted to the gun in his daughter's face. Suma grabbed her husband to hold him back. This chain reaction of concern muddled the official's attention and placed a measure of risk on each member of the chain.

The official turned back to the Abimbola.

"What's the matter, girl," he taunted, "do you love him?"

Abimbola blurted, "Yes."

This caught the official off guard. He regained control immediately by continuing his icy, even tone

"Maybe I should shoot you instead of him."

"Please don't," Abimbola whimpered as though her resistance had broken.

"You had better not!" shouted Issa.

This drew the official's attention and gun into Issa's face.

"I don't care about you or your family," he said in a low voice, as if he were only speaking to Issa.

"As a matter of fact, you are in my way."

He cocked the gun's hammer.

"Maybe I should kill *you* here and now."

"Please, leave my family alone," Suma cried out in desperation.

The official then moved to her face.

"My, you are a good woman," the official said with a devious smile as though they had just finished having sex.

"Get away from my wife," Issa directed as though his turn with the gun were still ahead of him.

"M-m-m," came a delicious sound from the official as he felt the strands of Suma's hair. Slowly his fingers moved down from her hair to the back of her neck and then slide down her front into her cleavage and under her breast.

Issa could not stand any more of this debasing behavior. He jerked free from his detainer, leapt over to his wife, and grabbed the official's throat.

The sudden move caught the official unaware, and he fell to the ground with the gun tossed to one side, and Issa on top of him slugging him in the face with one punch after another.

The guards instantly released their prisoners in order to get Issa off the official and into handcuffs as quickly as possible. It took two on each arm to stop Issa. It took one more guard to get the cuffs on him.

Meanwhile, the official pulled out a white handkerchief to wipe blood and sweat from his face. He then reached over to pick up his gun and wipe it off as well.

"Take him away!" he commanded as the guards continue to wrestle a defiant Issa to the vehicle.

Once inside, two guards stayed with Issa while three came back for Sydney.

Suma and the girls stood crying for their men who were being taken away.

Then Issa turned to his family and instructed, "Suma, go to see the pastor. It's not safe here."

The official then turned to Suma and warned her, "I'll be back for you and the girls, later."

She leered at him, not giving him any sign of fear. She was afraid, but she would not show it until the ruthless government people were gone.

With the men in the two trucks, their engines were started, headlights turned on, and their steering wheels aimed toward the jail. As the trucks turned around to head back to the city, the headlights caught flashed images of Suma standing near the hut entrance with her arms around her two younger daughters as her older daughter stood a step away reaching toward the vehicles.

CHAPTER

24

With only the red taillights showing, Suma said to her girls, "Let's go inside the hut." As they ran inside, Suma began to pace back and forth. Then she looked up to the stars and said out loud, "Now what do I do, Father?"

As if reply, she heard the wild beasts beyond the fields, in the jungle cover. Long ago she had learned of the dangers of traveling by night, even with the protection of torches and a gun—protection she did not have.

"What is worse, Father, being eaten by wild beasts or being attacked by guards? How do I protect my family?"

As Suma paced back and forth, a Psalm welled up inside her.

It was Psalm 91: "Those who live in the shelter of the Most High will dwell in the shadow of the Almighty."

She stopped, pondered, and then started pacing again.

"You will not be afraid of the terror by night or the pestilence that stalks in darkness."

She again stopped, pondered, and then started pacing again.

"For you have made the Lord your refuge even the Most High your dwelling place."

She again stopped, pondered, and then started pacing again.

"No evil will befall you and no disaster will come near your tent."

She turned and eyed her hut, wondering how much a tent it might be. But tents could be packed and moved; huts were not built for any travel. She wrung her hands and then started pacing again.

"For God will give his angels to guard you in all your ways. You will tread upon lion and cobra."

She did not want to look down or think what might be moving in the ditch alongside the paths or roadway nearby.

"Tents," she muttered and turned to walk into hers.

"Mom, I am so scared," Aba whimpered as she rushed to hug her mother.

"So am I, sweetheart. So am I," she said in as much of a reassuring tone as she could muster.

"Mom, I am so sorry for doing this to you and dad," Abimbola said with tears welling up in her eyes. She wanted to hug her mother, but Aba seemed attached to Suma and very much in the way.

"Girls," Suma said while trying to look each one in the eye. "What I would like for you to do is to gather everything that is important to you and put it in a bag. Things not in your bag will be left behind here. And remember, whatever you fit in your bag, you will need to carry it for a distance. So don't make your bag too heavy."

"Mom," Amia cut in, "are the men going to get us?"

"Not if I can help it," Suma replied. "Let's pray for each other and for your dad."

Suma's prayer was pointed but brief. Then the girls and Suma went to their spaces to pack.

***

Suma awoke rather sore and cold. It took only a moment to recall that she and the girls were outside their hut hidden from the path and roadway at night, but now highlighted by the early morning sun that had just broken over the horizon.

She looked around her. The girls were still sleeping. They were huddled into a dog pile, keeping each the other warm. Suma's Bible rested on her lap along with a flashlight, whose light was now weak. She put both items into her bag.

Her plan had worked. She thought that if the guards had returned during the night, they would have searched the hut. And not seeing them, they would have assumed that they were on the road and would have driven their vehicles quickly away. She thought it unlikely that they would take the time to search the backside of the hut. Anyway, it was what she took from the psalm that had come to her the night before.

She knelt on the ground and thanked God for protection through the night: "Thank you, God, for your protection and faithfulness over my family and me. Keep Issa safe."

The girls were still asleep. What a shame, she thought, to have to wake them so early. But they needed to move now that daylight was close upon them.

"Girls, it's time to go," she whispered. "I want you to be as quiet as you can be."

Their eyes opened, and they mumbled, "Yes, mom," perhaps even before they had taken in her message. Slowly they got their bags reassembled. Then they looked at the hut one more time before running away.

***

The roadway took them past the older man's empty village. He had heckled the family as they passed by many times. Yet, this morning something was different. Instead of rushing over to them, he was in a garden, working. Instead of matted hair, he wore dread locks that were neat and tidy. Instead of a scruffy beard, he was clean-shaven. Instead of filthy smelly clothing, he was dressed in a suit—with a tie, in a garden?

Perhaps the most surprising thing for Suma was that he didn't rush over in a wild manner to threaten or berate them. Instead, he looked up from his hoe and said, "Ladies, it is not good to travel alone in the early morning."

"Then come with us," Suma beckoned him, as she noticed movement on the roadway ahead. "A truck is coming in the distance—with its lights on," she called to the old man.

"Then, ladies, come over here," the old man called while using one arm and hand to make a welcoming or "come here" motion. He helped the women get behind a large bush quickly, without being spotted. "Wait right here," he cautioned them, "I need to get something."

The truck was moving quickly for the road condition, and it did not slow down when approaching the old man's abandoned village. It rumbled past the large bush without any hesitation. Then Suma heard the reason. The men were laughing as if they were drunk. And a bottle landed in the ditch. She was right; they were drinking.

As the truck and its dust cloud thundered in the distance, the old man returned with a shotgun. "We'll need this for our trip," he reassured Suma.

Without calculating its danger, Suma replied, "Then bring that too. As long as you don't shot *us* with it."

They started to walk down the roadway. "We must move quicker," he motioned, and the group picked up its pace. Even so, the man stayed by Suma's side as they shuffled their feet along at nearly a jogging pace. Without water or practice at this, she wondered how long the girls and she could keep up this pace. But they kept it going for one mile, then another.

Finally, they needed to rest.

The old man located some brush they could sit behind to avoid being seen from the road. Suma looked at the old man in his suit carrying only a shotgun. What a sight. She wanted to ask him how and why he had changed.

And, he seemed like he wanted to talk about it. After catching his breath, he spoke.

"Something happened to me last night, and I want to share it with you," he began. "I got changed by God."

"Oh-h," Suma said. "You mean the suit?"

"No, much deeper than that. I got awakened last night, and I felt the need to pray. I haven't felt that in a long time. And as I was praying I looked over at your hut, and I saw such amazing things."

Suma was still breathing heavily and was really too tired to keep up her side of the conversation. So she merely nodded, and the old man kept talking.

"Well, I saw angels overhead. God was with you, protecting you. And I haven't witnessed that in a long time—well, before my wife died. You see, I used to be a pastor before my wife died. When she died, I guess I lost my faith. And I lost my mind. I became bitter toward God. I was bitter until last night."

She thought a prayer of thanks and nodded again.

"So, last night," he continued, "I saw angels circling your hut. And this prompted me to pray for your safety. But then I fell asleep. It was a fitful sleep. And when I awoke, I had the sudden urge to pray for your village. I felt a heavy burden to pray because I felt an intense burden, like the sun and moon were being blotted out and the grass was turning to dust. I knew that a family was in extreme danger."

Suma could now speak.

"I was afraid, but I had peace. I know that this sounds strange."

"Well, I could not go back to sleep," the old man continued. "So I got up and prayed all night and my bitterness was gone by morning."

"My husband was arrested last night," Suma was finally able to explain.

"Then you will not be able to go back to your village. It will be destroyed," the old man said with soulful regret. "But," he cheered up, "everything will work out for your good. You will see."

Then he laughed as though he were mocking the evil government; their due was coming.

"Thank you, so much, for your prayers and vigil over us. We also appreciate your coming with us now."

"Well, that's because you are going to see my son."

"Who is your son?" Suma asked.

"Your pastor."

"You? You are the pastor's father? We have heard so much about you. We have been praying for you for quite some time. But I imagined that you had moved to a different mission field."

"Well," the old man said, "I have been in a very crazy place for a long time. Sort of like I wasn't here."

"You're a prophet."

"Yes, what I tell you is true. Things will work out for your good."

"Your son will be glad to see you. I know you miss your wife, but has your mourning ended now?"

"I do miss my wife, but I must help others. That is what she would want me to do. So, I will get you and your daughters to my son's place safely."

"And you have such special abilities to encourage many people, as your promise makes true for us. Thank you," Suma replied.

She looked into his eyes and smiled. He looked into her eyes and returned a smiling confidence.

***

The military truck was parked near Issa and Suma's hut. Some guards stood by with lighted torches. Other guards rushed inside and around the hut. Still others were quickly inspecting other empty huts in the village. The commander stood next to the government official who was enraged.

"Where are they?" he demanded.

"They're gone?" the commander said as though he were surprised at this turn of events.

"Of course they're gone," the official retorted. "It took you nearly 12 hours to come back to grab the woman and her daughters."

"Sir, it's not my fault that we had a flat tire."

"Flat tire? My ass. Your men have been drinking. I can smell it on their breath. And some of them are still not able to focus effectively."

The commander shrugged his shoulders as though this were news to him. Although he had not been drinking, he knew what despicable things his men had been—he had been—forced to do.

"Do I have to come with you to oversee every-thing?" the official complained. Then he turned to the guards and shouted, "Burn it! Burn that hut! Burn all the huts. I want this village leveled right now."

"But sir, shouldn't we check each hut first? People might still be in them."

"I don't care about having any civilian witnesses survive. I want everyone in this region to fear me and not resist me. They can be machete-ed, burned, or shot. And I don't care which."

The dry thatched grasses in each hut easily caught fire. As one hut after another was set ablaze, the dark smoke curled its way into the heavens. It smelled to the commander like burnt sesame oil, used in Asian dishes he had once enjoyed when times were more relaxed and riches passed around more. But now it smelled like death to him.

***

Suma, her girls, and the old man were again walking briskly along the roadway, watching for any vehicles that might come from either direction. Because they were walking away from the hut, they did not see the dark curl of smoke rising above their village, their home. Perhaps that was a good thing for when the old man saw it and pointed it out to them, he said, "Everything is gone now—everything."

"There's no going back," Suma said in agreement.

CHAPTER

25

Outside Feury's club, people had endured political scandals, such as Watergate, the bitter end of U.S. involvement in Vietnam, and the resignation of President Richard M. Nixon. Inside, Feury wanted each patron to have a good time. He also liked discovering new talent, especially black talent.

His club supported new or younger jazz musicians and singers whenever possible. Of course, the Duke Ellingtons and Ella Fitzgeralds were still drawing the concert crowds. Yet Feury wanted to discover and promote the next generation—give his club that special note: He already had several notable successes. For example, "The Summer Knows" was first played here by Michel Jean Legrand, the music writer.

Most of the time, however, Feury's budget depended on regular, on-stage talent. Tonight one of his regulars was singing contemporary favorites—music the crowd could hum or sing or use as the launching point to reminisce.

Feury sat at his usual table with his usual drink, de-fizzed Coca Cola in a red wine glass. He needed his edge to keep the patrons' experience at its best. He scanned the room. The crowd was full—every table with two or more persons, and even the tough-looking men had gorgeous women on their arms—and nicely dressed: two signs that tonight's cash take would be better than average. The bar area's tables were also full with men slipping away down the hall and returning later.

Beside him, Chijioke sat drinking a single malt scotch with a single ice cube that he was swishing around in his glass to the beat. Feury eyed him and smiled. Chijioke had turned out to be a good friend, someone who wanted to learn the ways of money and someone who brought money to the table. If Feury had a friend, then it might be Chijioke.

Suddenly a gasp arose near the door and wave of shock rattled through the crowd. Feury quickly moved through his group of patrons to the action's center. New York policemen were standing in a swarm near the door. In front of them was a man in a dark, somewhat cheap suit. Feury spotted the leader and approached him.

"Excuse me, but what's this all about?" Feury asked in a kind, but firm voice.

"We have a search warrant for the owner."

"I'm the owner. What is this for?"

"We are authorized to search the premises for illegal drugs."

"Well, I don't have any drugs here. Mine is a reputable establishment," he replied in a firm, but steely tone, attempting to cover the anger rising in his body.

The detective handed over the paperwork while several policemen pushed past Feury and walk toward the bar side of the establishment. Quickly other policemen then pushed past and moved toward the left side and moved through the restaurant tables toward the stage area.

"Reputable? Not according to our captain."

"Captain Sebastian Smith is a racist bigot. He doesn't like it that a black man owns a very successful night club south of Harlem. Look around and see for yourself. Smith has been trying to close me for the past two years."

"Well, sorry then, sir, but our captain wants us in here. You'll just need to step aside."

"And there's not a damn thing I can do about it?"

"That's correct, sir."

"Hey, I pay my taxes."

"Then, I suggest you take our performance up with the mayor."

"Yah, right. He's just as corrupt."

Feury motioned for his staff to clean up, and they instantly moved in every direction as if they had run this fire drill a dozen times. Some patrons started to leave while others needed to check out first. Everyone moved toward an exit and left.

Feury strode straight back to his table to where Chijioke sat innocently. "Chijioke, if you are not a citizen of this country, I suggest you leave immediately through the route we discussed."

Without hesitation, Chijioke stood from his chair, straightened his suit and tie, and marched directly to the stage area, ducked through the back curtains. Then he shoved the crash bar exit-door open. He looked back for a moment. Police had not yet made it this far in their search. He peered out the door to see if police were already stationed outside. He saw no one waiting, in a police uniform or in plain clothes. He walked out the backstage door, turned right onto the sidewalk, and walked at a brisk, steady pace. He heard the door close again and again. Other patrons must have followed me, he thought.

***

A whistle sounded. "Hey, you. Stop!"

Chijioke knew better than to obey this directive. He ducked down a side alley and started to run. Toward the other end of the alley, Chijioke realized that other police may be coming up that street. He had passed a dumpster. He knew his plan wouldn't work if the police were watching both ends of the alley. But...

Chijioke looked inside the dumpster. It seemed to be mostly empty boxes. He thought about his suit, then his life in America, and ... he swung himself into the dumpster and behind the boxes.

Now the cover. He hadn't thought to arrange it beforehand. Fortunately, it was leaning against the building wall. All he had to do was slowly lower it to close the dumpster. Then he settled in.

The first thing he noticed was that he had misjudged the dumpster's contents. Under the boxes were bags of trash and garbage. This stuff hadn't put there that evening. It must have come from an Indian restaurant. The smell of curry and vegetables now rotting brought up a gagging response. Well, good thing he had already eaten, he thought.

The second thing he noticed was that the evening was cold. He rubbed his hands together and wondered whether his body heat would give him away—or how long he could stay in the dumpster, if the searchers lingered in the alley.

Then he heard footsteps coming toward him at a run. His heart raced. While he didn't want to spend all night in this dumpster, he surely didn't want to be found like this. Not now.

A muffled command filtered through the metal box's garbage and a dog whimper. With a dog sniffing, he hardly stood a chance of escape. But again, Chijioke held to his plan.

The dog handler had led his charge past every dumpster in the alley. The trail always stopped at this one. But the dog had not begun barking or sitting down as if the suspect had been located. Next to this dumpster was a fire escape. Had the suspect used the dumpster to grab the bottom rung on the escape and climb to the roof? Well, he had better check out the dumpster, just in case.

The cover creaked open as the policeman lifted the lid. He scanned his flashlight back and forth. He spotted boxes on top and then the wretched smell of old restaurant toss outs. Who could tolerate such a stink? he thought to himself. He closed the lid and radioed back to his commander about the trail and the fire escape.

A long time later, Chijioke thought that every bar must have served its last call and that every patron had gone home. His hands were numb, and he could no longer smell the stink. It must be time for him to go home as well.

He lifted the dumpster lid a few inches and looked around. No one. Then he slowly shifted his weight and stood up, again resting the lid on the building's wall behind it. He put one foot on the boxes to test whether he could climb up again on this stack without making too much noise. The stack held. Then he neatly swung himself over the top and onto the alley.

He looked at his suit. Garbage stains everywhere and a few pieces of carrot peeling and lettuce and … he didn't want to think about it. This suit was ruined, but he needed to get to his apartment. A hefty tip should cover the inconvenience, he thought. So he walked out to the street and hailed a cab.

Once in and underway, the driver looked in the rearview mirror. What was that smell, he wondered. He sniffed. It surely was an Indian curry, and he had picked up his fare near a good restaurant. But he couldn't image how this man would have eaten so much of it or come to smell so bad. He lifted one hand and put a finger on each side of his nose. Then he looked back again, caught the eyes of his fare, and made a stinky sign while saying nothing.

Chijioke was embarrassed—and concerned that the cabbie's recollection would be a little too clear and distinct. Maybe taking a cab had been a mistake? Well, he couldn't reconsider at this stage. He needed to get home, take a long shower, and bury this suit somewhere.

When he got out of the cab, as planned he paid the fare and then gave the cabbie a generous tip. With all the cabbies in New York, he comforted himself with the thought that he would likely never to see this cabbie again.

Then he needed to confront the doorman, someone he had seen and would continue to see nearly every night—at about this time. As the door was opened, Chijioke said to the doorman, "Very bad accident at a restaurant" and walked to the elevator.

Once inside his apartment, Chijioke carefully took off each piece of clothing and, using two dry cleaning bags, he had placed one inside the other. Then he assembled the entire suit on a hanger, pulled the bags over the hanger, and securely tied first the inner bag and then the outer bag. At the top, he used tape to seal the bags shut.

Now, what to do with the drugs in his pockets? He decided to put them in a drugstore bag he found in his kitchen. (Not that he could remember needing anything from a legitimate pharmacy, but his housekeeper kept everything and probably even left her bags among his things.)

That done, he turned on his shower, brought a variety of soaps and washes with him, and lathered and scrubbed until he felt clean again. It was a long shower.

While getting dressed, he heard police sirens at his apartment. Quickly, he finished dressing, grabbed his "dry cleaning" and drugstore bags, and headed down the stairway. At the main floor, the stairway gave an option of walking through the lobby or exiting directly to the top level of the resident parking ramp. He headed toward the ramp.

Not far away, he spotted trash cans. He stuffed his dry cleaning into one receptacle and his drugstore bag into the other. Then he walked through the ramp and onto the street. Even though the early morning air was chilly, he found it a nice morning for a long walk. Hopefully, he could bypass police and avoid a lineup.

CHAPTER

26

After his summer in upstate New York working as a director's assistant, Abdalla had enough cash to begin his courses with books and basic equipment he needed for his movie-creating craft. The mugging had left him short, but Chijioke had covered some of that loss. Yet Abdalla wanted to repay his brother and perhaps build up a bigger cushion of cash.

His hours at McDonald's during the week and his weekend position as a doorman at the hotel met his on-going living expenses. Unlike the restaurant clean-up job, which was some distance from his apartment, the hotel was nearby. His hours at the hotel were the graveyard shift, which meant few opportunities to earn large tips. Even so, the hotel did afford him some time to read and study, as it had this evening.

A limousine approached the hotel driveway, and Abdalla began to play the tip game even when his peers were not present. The limo was not a cheap stretch job that brides or grooms rented to be whisked from one bar to another. It was the finest in appointments and wasn't too long or gaudy. A point. Then he caught a woman's face in the rear seat and she was over 40 years old. Two more points. Then he added in the time of night; she would be anxious to have her travels over and rest in her room. Another point; four out of five. This fare should result in a substantial tip.

He approached the car as it was coming to a stop. As soon as it halted, he grasped the door handle and carefully opened the door. As he examined her closely, he spotted an expensive necklace of diamonds under a coat with mink on the collar. Five for five, he thought.

She extended her hand for assistance. As Abdalla carefully turned his palm upward to offer his hand, he notice that she wore a diamond bracelet and ring. Her hands were well manicured, as one might expect, but her skin was supple, like calf's skin he thought. Her fingertips were also pure as though they had done lit- tle—and he thought, perhaps, no—work.

Hand-in-hand, she swiveled her hips and legs in unison, planted her feet on the driveway, tugged on Abdalla for a pull upward, and said in the sweetest, Southern voice, "Got my bags, boy."

Even though Africans had had a different struggle than African Americans—Africans had had black oppressors more than white—the economic part of their struggles was quite similar. Corrupt govern- ments, Abdalla knew, could strip-mine minerals or opportunities. Denial of education was often used to keep classes (or races) of persons poor and dependent.

All of this went through his mind when he heard the word *boy*. Without thinking, he squeezed her soft hand. Then he shook his head, maybe to show off his dread locks under his uniformed hat, and said, "Yes, Madam." Then he helped her to the door.

He pulled the hotel door open with one hand while he gracefully motioned with the other that she should move through the doorway.

Once she was safely inside, he went to the back of the limo and got her bags. To one side, he set a smaller bag so that he could lift out the larger bags at the bottom of the trunk.

A young man approached from behind. The lights overhead showed him to be a teenager, disheveled— perhaps from sleeping under overpasses or in the park. Had any of the staff been paying attention, they would have spotted him as trouble. Had the wind come from behind the young man, Abdalla might have even smelled him approaching. No one paid attention—until just a couple of steps from the trunk. The young man took two quick steps, grabbed the exposed small bag, and kept running into the dimly illumined street and then alley.

When Abdalla turned his attention back to the trunk, he saw the bag missing and the young man carrying it off down the street. "Hey, watch these other bags!" he commanded the driver, who had been confused by the action. Abdalla darted down the street in pursuit of the stolen bag.

He ran until he could no longer determine which way the young man had gone next. He looked down one street and then down an alley. Nothing. No sound. No movement. Abdalla stood silently, holding his breath as he had done often when hunting game back in Africa. Nothing.

Realizing that his search had come to an end, he walked briskly back to the hotel.

By this time, the driver had gotten all the other bags from the trunk and given them to a bell hop just inside the door.

Abdalla arrived just as a small group approached the door, and he opened the door for them. Then a car pulled up into the driveway, and Abdalla assisted them. Then the lobby lounge must have closed, and a few tippy patrons needed assistance operating the door on their way out. Then another car and a few more bags.

Life was pretty much back to usual—except that Abdalla had not gotten any tips.

Some time later, the manager appeared at the door. "Abdalla, can I see you inside my office?"

Abdalla understood that this question required only that he go to the manager's office, but he automatically said, "Yes, sir." They went inside together.

The Southern guest sat in one chair facing the desk. She had attempted to reposition the chair so that it looked more out the window toward the lobby. Then she shifted her weight in the chair from one side to another by crossing her legs this way and then that. Finally positioned, she poised her right hand over her chin and tapped it lightly as if planning what to shift next.

While Abdalla hung his coat and hat, the manager walked behind the hotel's front desk to return to his office and slip along the narrow pathway in behind his desk. Through the door window, he saw the woman—and he saw his office with fresh eyes. Unlike all the luxurious selections of stone, fabric, and gold throughout the hotel, unlike the feeling of space and grandeur, this room was small, cramped, and rather dreary; it looked worn. And, if what the woman claimed were true, then Abdalla was in serious trouble. The woman appeared to be influential. He had worked too hard to get to this position.

He should have held this meeting in one of the much nicer business rooms or not held it at all. After all, he could simply believe the guest and terminated Abdalla. But, he recalled another incident. One employee had accused another of taking too much break time. Abdalla had stepped forward with facts, but in doing so, Abdalla had to reveal that he had taken a longer break in order to get warm. The manager admired Abdalla truthfulness in that situation and was inclined to trust Abdalla in this situation as well.

"He'll be here in just a moment," the manager explained as he settled into his office chair. She just lifted her nose a bit, as if giving a nod, well, perhaps a condescending nod, he thought.

Abdalla opened the door and entered.

"Abdalla, please sit," the manager said, pointing to the other chair, the one next to the woman. "Close the door, if you will."

As instructed, Abdalla sat in the remaining chair—next to the woman.

"*I* don't want *him* sitting next to *me*," she intoned.

"Because I'm black?"

"Nothing of the kind. Because you are a thief who has taken my treasures."

The manager saw everything unraveling. To the woman, he said, "Okay, I'll have him stand." And to Abdalla, he said, "There seems to be a problem."

"A *very large* problem," the woman corrected.

"Abdalla, this guest says one of her bags is missing."

"It was *stolen*, and *he* is *guilty*."

"She says, Abdalla, that you stole it."

"Oh, no, sir."

"*I* told you, *he* would *deny* it."

Abdalla now standing turned to the woman, "I did not steal anything."

"Our guest says it was on the ground when she got out of the limo, but now it is gone."

"As I was getting the bags out of the limo, I…"

She interrupted, "*Limousine*. It was a *limousine*."

"Yes, ma'am."

"Please finish, Abdalla," the manager pleaded.

"…I saw a teen-ager running away from the hotel. I thought to chase after him, but he got away."

"A *likely* story."

"No, the teen must have taken the bag as I was helping the limo driver get the bags out of the trunk."

"*Limousine* driver."

"Did you see where he was going?"

"He was running East."

"There was *over* a *million* dollars of *jewels* in that bag."

"Did you notice if the teen had anything in his hands?"

"No sir, I did not."

"Well, I am sorry to say this, Abdalla, but until this matter can be investigated by the police, you will not be able to work here. If you are found guilty of stealing this woman's jewels, she will press charges, and you will likely be imprisoned or deported back to Africa."

"But I did not take them!"

"Africa? Your *kind* needs to *go back* from whence you *came*."

"Ma'am, I'm sure this matter will be resolved and Abdalla found innocent."

"He's *guilty*, I *tell you*."

"Abdalla, turn in your uniform and clock out."

***

Abdalla hung his uniform in the locker, put on his own clothes, and gave his security badge to the manager. Out on the street, the morning was still dark as he shuffled down the sidewalk. A tear formed in his right eye. Then his left eye became blurry. Trying to see the tops of his shoes, he sighed and prayed.

"Father, I cannot go back to Africa when the vision you have given me remains unfulfilled. Please help me."

CHAPTER

27

At the center of the room hung a chandler made of crystals illuminated by lights shaped like flames. The rich carpeting had obviously been made for the floor; its design emphasized the square shape of the room, the center under the chandler was the only place where whites and golds were used in such generous patterns. Centered on all four walls were curtains that hung the entire height of 24 feet, floor to ceiling. On two walls were large doors centered between the curtains. On the other two walls were a window to the hallway and a mirror. The center carpet motif was drawn out with aisle ways from each door, window, or mirror to the center. Even the adjacent square template in the carpeting brought one's attention from any corner or side to the center.

The walnut inlaid table was not square, but rectangular, and was designed to arrest and hold the attention. Each side of the table held 12 chairs. Yet this table seemed tiny in this room. On it was a single pitcher of water on a gold tray, with only two glasses, one on each side. It could have been a banquet room at a prestigious New York hotel. But it was meeting room A at one of the largest and most successful investment firms in the City.

A single chair was pulled back for Chijioke's comfort. He had been escorted here, not by a receptionist, but by one of the partners. He looked around. Perhaps he should redo his apartment more like this, he thought. He had been with this investment firm since arriving in New York. He loved, not money, but what it brought. He turned over a glass and poured himself a drink of water. Ahh, the taste of success, he thought.

Two men entered and marched straight down the walkway toward Chijioke. Each carried a stack of papers and, for it only being 11 a.m., seemed haggard. He recognized the look from his heavier drug days. While taking sips, he watched them march down the aisle like two pages before royalty. Each wore a black suit with modest, yet colorful ties. Their shoes flashed streaks of light from the chandler and overhead lights. The only thing that really distinguished them, Chijioke thought, was that one was nearly bald while the other had curly locks of hair.

Upon arrival, each set his stack of papers neatly on either side of Chijioke.

Mister Bald said, "Hello, Mister Ndao. Thanks for coming to see us on such short notice."

"You said something about 'trouble'?"

"Well, one of your investments in which you placed a lot of money went, well, bankrupt."

"Which one?"

"It's the technology company in your portfolio; the only stock in your portfolio."

"Yes," Chijioke said, "I picked that one myself."

"Well, sir," Mister Curly said mournfully, pointing to the pile of papers he brought, "as our correspondence shows, we advised you—even begged you, wouldn't you say?" he looked toward Mister Bald, "to diversify your portfolio."

"The company was rocked by scandal," inserted Mister Bald.

The men waited for this news, if it was news, to sink in. Chijioke, however, gave no reaction.

The first man continued, "The president of the company was a corrupt, unethical president. The FBI caught him embezzling the company's money. So the FBI arrested the president and closed the company last night."

"Yes, I read about it in the *New York Times*. It seems all very sad. So, what does it mean for me?"

The two investment advisors looked at each other. Would they have to spell out this situation with simpler language? How could the implications not be plain?

Mister Curly said very slowly as though each word was an entire sentence, "This was the company in which you wanted us to keep your money..."

"*All* of your money..." interrupted Mister Bald.

"Yes, I asked you to do this. That is fine. So what does this mean?"

Mister Curly continued, "It means, sir, that your money is gone."

"Gone? How gone?"

"Well, all gone, sir," both said in unison.

Then, Mister Bald continued, "All of your money is completely gone."

And Mister Curly added, "You have no more money in your account with us."

"Are you telling me that all of my money has been taken?"

"Yes, sir."

"We have been trying to get a hold of you," Mister Curly said, while tapping his finger on the top of his stack of papers.

"We have been warning you for the past two months about this company," Mister Bald said, while he ran his thumb up and down his stack of papers.

As the men repeated themselves, Chijioke could not hear the words. Instead, he only heard the sound of glass crashing, as though the chandler had fallen on top of the water pitcher. He slowly rotated his body while his eyes looked at each detail in the room. He was shutting down as though his power cord had been unplugged.

"So, let me see if I understand. All my money is gone? I walked in here with several million, and I walk out penniless?"

"Yes, sir."

"Oh, my God! What am I going to do now?"

Chijioke then got up from his chair and walked out, muttering "It's gone" with each step he took.

CHAPTER

28

Not far from New York University and the Ukrainian Institute was an ethnic food vendor inside Central Park that served Polish sausages and Ukrainian dried fruit compote. It was one of perhaps a thousand food vendors who served their ethnic delicacies to those weary for a taste of home and others eager for a taste of elsewhere.

A father with four children gathered around the stand. He had ordered six sausage sandwiches and drinks—a real spurge. His wife and two more children were on a blanket, waiting for the treats to be delivered. The afternoon was sunny and pleasant, and they joined countless others for a break in the park.

Chijioke sat on a park bench, joined by others, because seating was tight this afternoon. He watched the vendor with cunning, much as he had when he hunted game back in Africa. Casually he approached the vendor's stand, looking like the next customer. As the vendor loaded one after another bun, Chijioke carefully pocketed one after another compote.

Then, hands in pockets, he turned and slowly walked away, looking for another bench. Later he would un-pocket his haul and devour as much as he could. He didn't quite know what "living hand to mouth" meant, but he imagined that this was pretty close.

***

The cab pulled up to the curb of the apartment building. Abdalla stepped out, reached into his pocket, and handed the driver fare plus a tip. It wasn't until after the cab drove away that he spotted his brother sitting on his apartment building's steps.

"Hey, where have you been, man?" Chijioke asked.

"At school, studying. Have you been waiting long?"

"For a while."

"I'm surprised to see you here."

"Yes, I am equally surprised to be here. But I've lost everything today."

"That is too bad for you."

"Yes, for me and all my friends. Now I have no money—and I have no one else to help me."

"What happened?"

"A company that I invested in went bankrupt. I had all my money in there, and now it's gone."

"Now I'm surprised again," Abdalla said to Chijioke. "I thought you said that you were going to save some. Did you save any money?"

"No, I invested it all in one place. And now it's all gone."

"So you are here…"

"I'm here because I need a place to stay for a while."

"How long?"

"Probably for several months. I need to develop a new plan and get some cash flowing again."

"Well, we'd need to clear it with the landlord, Chijioke. And frankly, I don't want you here if you continue selling drugs and whatnot. I just think it would be a bad idea for you to stay here longer than a night or two."

"I am finished selling drugs. And I won't do drugs anymore. Even if I wanted them, I could not get them now. My friends have all left me. And I am broke."

"Chijioke, you sent only a little money back to dad, mom, and the girls. Yet, now you are asking me, a poor student, for assistance to carry all your needs for several months? …" Abdalla took in the irony of this.

"Yes, I see your point. But please help me."

"There's one other thing," Abdalla said. "You are not the only one with bad news."

"Why, what else happened?"

"A rich lady had her bag of jewelry stolen while I was unloading her baggage from a limo. She claims that I have stolen her things. There will be a police investigation and, if I'm found guilty, I'll be imprisoned or deported back to Africa because I am not a citizen here." His eyes became puffy again and his tongue, thick. He paused, then he said, "Okay, come on. It's late."

Chijioke was relieved. He had survived his first day and night as a penniless man. Now he was almost back in the game.

***

The hallway in Abdalla's apartment was usually quiet at this late night hour. He slipped his key into the first lock and then the second and so on until he could open the door. The television sounded only louder: gun shots, a siren, and the screeching of tires. If the television had not come with the apartment, Abdalla would never have purchased one. It had so little to do with his dreams and aspirations. Of course, he would surely direct made-for-television movies and shows. But that was the outcome, and watching television was not the means to achieve such an outcome.

As he stepped through the doorway, he saw dishes piled higher than the gooseneck faucet. The door under the sink was open and the trash can sitting on the floor, surrounded by food wrappers and debris from who knew what. The kitchen table had newspapers laying on it.

Stepping in farther, he scanned the remainder of the small apartment. His bedspread was still neatly arranged on his bed. Nearby was a portable bed with the covers piled at one end and the pillow on the floor.

Then his eyes came to Chijioke, sprawled on the easy chair, watching some waste-of-time program. He was sitting almost sideways in the chair with his head propped on one stuffed armrest and his legs dangling over the other armrest. On his stomach was an open bag of chips with fragments on the chair and floor.

"Chijioke? How long have you been watching television?"

"For a while, I guess."

"And just how long is 'a while'?"

"For a few hours."

"Did you look for a job today?"

"Yeah. I looked for a while, and then I came back."

"I see you didn't take out the trash."

"I guess I forgot."

"Chijioke, I go to school all day, and I work a part-time job every weekday. I have to replace lost income from my second with savings from my summer job. And I come home and see you making a mess while watching television?"

Chijioke didn't reply. Instead he took a chip, placed it on his tongue, and then crunched it and swallowed. "Say, what are these?" he asked. "They're good."

"I'm sorry, Chijioke, but I cannot support you anymore."

"What does that mean?"

"Look, Chijioke, I got a letter from mom today. She told me some very bad news. The girls cannot go to school because the money has all run out. All their resources are gone. I'm not sure what dad was doing quietly with the diamonds was right. But you had a hand in disrupting his life through your diamond sales. And yet, you sit here doing nothing!"

"Tomorrow, I will look harder for a job. Tomorrow."

"You are depleting my funds. I cannot keep feeding and taking care of you. You are so lazy!"

"Lazy?" Chijioke repeated.

That hurt, he thought. This assessment surely could not be correct.

"All you do is sit around, eat, sleep, and watch television—and create trash."

"But no one wants to hire me."

"That's because you look like a thug."

"Wait a minute. Thug? I was with the wealthiest people here in New York City! I dined with many socially upper-class people. They accepted me."

"Well, maybe they can accept you back now and support you because I cannot support you, me, and our family back home."

"Abdalla, you could just stop sending money back to them. Maybe that would ease your burden."

"I have only been able to send a little. But I cannot believe what you are suggesting. You think *only* about yourself and your easy life."

"Well, that's not quite true. We should help people we care about. Mom, I care about, but dad not so much."

"Do you know that our family back home is starving? Actually going without something to eat? All their food and resources are gone."

"I didn't know, but I really don't care."

"This is your family, Chijioke."

"Why do you think I left Africa?"

"To focus on yourself and make money."

"That's right, make money. I promised myself I would never again work hard like we did in Africa! I broke my back there, and dad was the task master."

"Well, I'm still breaking my back for you!"

"I'm not going to live in that poverty again. And I won't go back."

"Chijioke, you don't have anything. You're homeless without me. You don't have to go back, but if you want to stay here in America, you must work."

Then Abdalla thought to appeal to his brother's vision side.

"You. You, Chijioke, can achieve the American dream!"

"But I have to work hard?"

"That's right, now you do."

"I'm not going to sweep floors at McDonalds. Cleaning up after people is degrading work."

"I do it every day so you can enjoy a bag of chips. If you want to stay here with me, you have got to get a job and pay half of the expenses. And no dealing drugs."

Chijioke grabbed the bag and swung to a sitting position on the chair.

"I'm not going to put up with these sorts of demands!" he retorted.

"Look, Chijioke, we all have to pay our dues sometime."

"Mine have already been paid."

And with that, Chijioke stood up, threw the bag of chips on the chair, and stomped his feet toward the door. Then he unlocked the door, stepped over the threshold, and slammed the door shut.

As Abdalla again surveyed his apartment, he wondered if he had been too simplistic in his assessment of his brother. Chijioke was not merely lazy; he could also be stubbornly stupid. Where else would he go at this hour?

CHAPTER

29

Abdalla sat on a bench near his school holding a new letter from his mother. He did not notice the pigeons pecking for food or the sounds of children playing. Pollen from the trees and grass gave him a sniffle, but he didn't detect it. The news from home was simply overwhelming.

Another man sat down on the bench seat next to Abdalla, put his hands behind his head, and took a deep breath. "Nice day we're having," he said to Abdalla.

"I guess."

"That didn't sound very convincing."

"You are correct, sir. My family in Africa is having real trouble. My father was jailed by a corrupt government official, and we have lost our home—it was set ablaze and burned to the ground. And I might go to jail, because I am falsely accused, and then be sent back to Africa. All my dreams are, how do you say, flushed down the toilet."

Normally, Abdalla would have been much more reserved. But he knew this man.

"What part of Africa?"

"Senegal. Actually, the Casamance region in the South."

"Say, you look familiar to me," the man said. "Do I know you from somewhere?"

"Of course, you know Chijioke, my only brother."

"Chijioke Ndao is your brother?"

"Yes, but I do not know where he is. We had a huge fight the other night, and I think I have lost him for good. He must now be walking the streets."

"Well, I don't know where he is, either. Say, you're a student here, correct?"

"Yes, I'm in the spring semester of my junior year."

"And you're in the film directing program. Right?"

"Yes. I want to be a director. I have a film that I will be directing this summer. It would be nice to make it a feature, but I don't have the funds to do this."

"How much do you need?"

Abdalla drew his thumb and pointing fingers down his jaw bone.

"It takes millions of dollars to bring a film project into the theaters. And this can be risky, but usually each film brings back so much more."

"Maybe I can help. I've recently sold my club at a considerable profit. So I have money; I'm an investor looking for a risk and an adventure."

"Hmm. Forgive my forthrightness, but I thought you were a drug dealer."

"Oh, no. I was a club owner. I had partners who divided the club, and they used the backrooms. But, I didn't get involved with that. I stayed out front with the performers. Discovering talent—that has been my career. What I'm looking for is a fresh start in a new field. What I'm looking for is to invest in you."

"You would help me, a complete stranger?"

"Come on, you're not a complete stranger. I've met you at the hotel and in my club. And I know your brother. Why, I could even help your family," Feury said, nodding toward the letter Abdalla was holding.

"How could you help them?"

Feury thought as he stretched his arms and back into the bench.

"I could bring them here. Yes, that would be a helpful move. I have some connections in the U.S. and Senegal governments. Your family could stay in my summer home on Staten Island."

"You're kidding, right?"

"No. I am serious."

"Then this is of God."

"Well, I think of it more this way: I help you with your film and family, and you give me a large percentage of the profits."

"I cannot promise you what you will get back, but you've got a deal!"

Then Abdalla carefully re-folded the letter from his mother, put it in his pocket, picked up his books, and headed to the library. He needed to research contracts and film profit-share percentages.

CHAPTER

30

The church, an old clapboard structure, never seemed as welcoming and safe as when Suma, the girls, and the old man arrived. The pastor and his wife were not surprised to see them at the door, but were surprised to see the old man—really the pastor's father, the prophet—with them and his protective shotgun. They had huddled in prayer, each taking a place on the wooden benches. As they finished their individual prayers of thanksgiving and help, the pastor led them in a communal prayer of thanksgiving and praise.

"Suma," the pastor said, "I'm so glad you are here. God will give you the direction you need."

"Suma, as I was praying," the old prophet said, "the Lord wanted me to tell you that your days in Africa are numbered. You need to prepare for a huge undertaking. God will open a door for you to go to another country."

"Why don't you go and get some sleep, Suma"? the pastor's wife said as she hugged Suma. "You're safe here."

"But I must go see my husband," Suma objected. "His time in jail must be very difficult for him. Please I must first go…"

"Why don't you do that later, Suma?" the pastor's wife continued. "He will understand."

"Oh, my. I have no money by which to get him out of jail," Suma realized.

"Suma, you need some rest," the pastor's wife said again.

"Perhaps you are right," Suma said to the woman. "Perhaps I do need to rest a bit."

***

Abdalla was in his bed, sleeping, when he had a dream.

This is his film premier with all of his family: his father and mother, his only brother, and his three younger sisters. The show has not yet begun. He stands in front of the curtain that shields the screen. He thanks his family; he thanks his investor. Then he sits down. He is sitting with his family, his mom and dad on either side; his sisters are in the row behind them. The curtain pulls to the sides, and they watch the movie together and enjoy themselves.

Abdalla awoke with a start and began to smile. He was with his family, watching the film he directed. He was with his family; life was good.

***

The warm day with its clear sky clear could have been taken for summer, even though it actually was late spring. White chairs were clustered in small groups around the pool area. Trays next to the chairs offered fancy, colorful drinks. The pool's water remained perfectly calm and inviting. Servants stood ready to handle any particular need—a drink refill, a dry towel, or a deep-tissue back rub. Abdalla could not believe that this was Feury's Staten Island summer home.

"I never asked you, but how did you get from Africa to the United States. You do have a green card, don't you?"

"Yes, my student visa permits me to work in the U.S. My pastor in Africa knew a missionary here in the U.S., Pastor John, and he helped me get into school."

"Well, your pastor must be a great guy. I guess, I'm not used to people helping others without some kind of strings attached."

"My pastor is always helping others. Now, about your comment: It makes me wonder why you are helping me."

"Well, I think it's pretty clear. I want to make money in the movie industry."

"Oh, that makes you as wise an investor as my brother. I did not know you knew how to produce movies."

"I don't. I just have money, and money talks, my friend."

"Yes, money talks as long as you have a large enough wad."

"By the way, speaking of money talking, I took care of that problem with your dad."

***

The prison guard's smile beamed as he scratched the back of his neck. Where else but in Africa? he thought. He held the briefcase, but kept the lid shut tight. He had already peeked inside and seen the stacks of bills. This was a good day.

"Issa? Sydney?" he called. "Stand up, you are going home." When he got to their cell door, he unlocked it, gave them the largest grin, and told them to get moving. "You must have someone who really loves you. Now get your butts out of here."

Issa and Sydney gathered up their few things quickly and met the jailer at the cell door. When it was unlocked, he bowed deeply. "Gentlemen," he said articulating every syllable as though he were address-ing kings, "please, right this way." Then he followed them to the security gate and out into the lobby.

Here their treatment became even more bizarre. The guard at the desk and others were drinking and having a good time. Those in the lobby waiting to see detainees—they were also having a drink. Issa and Sydney were each offered what appeared to be a dark red wine. When they each took a sip, it tasted like de-fizzed Coca Cola. Issa grimaced after his sip, even though the drink was sweet, not sour. He liked his colas fresher and a little cooler.

"Yes," the guard at the desk laughed, "we had to serve you this according to the directions. I have no idea why someone would take a good drink and let the gas from it."

Then he stopped and moved his eyes both ways and his lips wide, but pursed, as if he were thinking.

"But then again," he said, "I don't any idea why someone would pay for your release!"

The crowd in the lobby roared as they agreed or hoisted their glasses for a mock toast.

As Issa and Sydney finished the little party and headed for the door, the lobby guard called out, "Next time, could you arrange also to have some chips?"

Issa had not time for frivolity; he only muttered to himself that freedom tasted cool and bubbly.

"I am not counting on a 'next time'."

***

Feury and Abdalla had not moved from the pool area, but instead had dinner served at an elegant table. The servants brought each course of dinner with service that would have rivaled any restaurant in the city.

"So, let's get back to discussing the film project."

Feury picked up a portion of a pat of butter with his butter knife and wiped the knife on a piece of roll.

"Now that I'm a big investor, on the hook for millions, what is our movie about?"

"Well," Abdalla said with a sincere smile, "it's about my experience in America."

"It's not a horror film, I hope."

"Oh no, it's not. But it is pretty close to one. More like 'science gone bad'."

"Oh, now you are taking the fun out of it."

CHAPTER

31

The police had interviewed the woman whose jewelry bag and jewels had been taken along with
Abdalla, the hotel guard at the doorway, the manager
on duty, and Abdalla again. They also noted that a
steady stream of complaints had come into the police
station from guests in the city. Their purses or wallets
had been lifted—often at the same hour in early
morning.

The insurance company had also followed up with
Abdalla on their own and warned him that they were
watching his bank account and spending patterns.
Neither had the case had been solved nor Abdalla's
name cleared. The file could have been labeled 'case
laid aside' for a time. Abdalla wondered, How does
one build trust in this world? Apart from Feury, no
one really vouched for him or his character, even after
working for the same manager for several years.

Much like a rodent in the city, the teen-ager
worked at night. He knew his way around in the

darkness and could out maneuver most any police officer. Since the robbery, he had stayed low because he knew that the amount of jewels in that case could spark a large search for him. The owner would want her precious jewels back, the insurance company would want to return what was insured rather than risk an inflated owner's assessment, and the mayor would want a potential embarrassment solved rather than linger on the books.

It's a good thing I work alone on the supply-side, he thought. His method of operation was nothing fancy or novel. He would usual grab purses; they often had cash. At this hour, many easy marks would have just paid a large bar bill—often with cash because they didn't want the total cost of the night to be known by others, especially a spouse.

Some purse snatchers would try in the first 30 minutes of the robbery any credit cards they could dig out. This could double the take, he figured, but at the risk of giving police an ATM photo or finger prints. He knew that he couldn't go to a restaurant or all-night liquor store because of video surveillance and because, at this hour, he often needed a fix of drugs. He knew he was too smelly and shaky to pull off a charming patron routine. The quick purse heist at the hotel was his signature move. He would wait in the shadows at an exclusive hotel—and he moved from one side of the City to the other so as to be unpredictable.

On this snatch, however, he had over shot. In the dim light and in his own attempts to walk a quiet, steady rush past the limo, he thought he had grabbed the lady's large purse, not her jewelry bag.

This was the reason he also avoided smash-and-grabs. He knew how to use a hoodie to cover his face, that wasn't the problem, and the haul could be significant. Turning hardware into cash, that's the trick. He would need to involve others—experts in the value of jewelry or gold or whatever emptied out of the case. This required an entire chain of trust he simply couldn't muster. "Keep the plan simple, the operation tight, and the payoff in cash," a drug buddy had told him. That made a lot of sense.

He held the jewelry bag inside his hoodie. It made him look pregnant, but it kept any chrome or sparkles from flashing in the dim alleyway lighting. He went to one side of the alley, ducked behind a dumpster, and light a cigarette. He didn't like meeting strangers, he was weary because putting this deal together took time. Oh, and another thing about cash: it was much less identifiable than this jewelry case. One look, and the wrong person would know instantly that he had stolen this.

He heard something and turned to look. A car drove into the alley with its lights on, but once past the sidewalk, killed them as it slowly moved toward him. After 10 seconds, which seemed to the teen like several minutes, two men opened their car doors and slowly got out—and carefully walked toward him. With a dim light behind the men, the teen could see that one was carrying a gun, possibly a shotgun or a semi-automatic.

The driver spoke. "Hey, kid, ya' got the stuff?"

"Sure, how about you?"

"We're ready. Let's see what we're looking at first."

Unsure, the teen unzipped his sweatshirt and exposed the jewelry case.

"Ouu…" the gunman said. "These are old fashion, but they can hold a lot of stuff."

The driver took the case from the teen, unfastened the latches, and carefully opened the cover. Even in the dim light, he could see that the case was a cornucopia of diamonds and precious jewels all in classic settings—each worth a lot of money.

The teen stood there nervously, anxiously waiting for his payoff.

"Actually, kid," the driver said, "we lied. We don't have the stuff on us. It's in the next car."

"What? Wait a minute," the teen said in a low, but forceful voice. "I took a big risk coming here. I trusted you. I showed you my hand. Now I want my stuff."

"Glad you're careful in who you trust, kid, because you can't trust everyone. We came to make sure you had the stuff. The next car will make the trade."

The teen's torso tightened, and it looked as though he might unleash a punch or two.

"Relax," the gunman said. "You'll get your stuff. We just can't have drugs driving around if the jewels weren't what you said. Your stuff is coming."

With this, the teen's body relaxed. He watched as the two men walked back to their car, got in, started the engine, and drove past him to exit out the other end of the alley.

Then the teen became angry at himself. He had taken a risk on his largest haul, and now he might end up with a dainty case instead of the drugs.

Then another car pulled into the alley and, like the first one, shut off its headlights, drove close to him, and then shut off its engine. Again two men slowly got out of the vehicle. Again, one had a gun. This time, however, the driver carried a case. He carefully set it on a cardboard box, unlatched the cover, and opened it. The teen peered inside. Here it was, just as they had promised.

Quickly the teen handed over the jewelry case to the driver. He then slammed the cover down on the case, flipped the latches into their locked position, and picked up the case. He would be out of here in a moment. The case was heavy so taking large strides was difficult, especially when he was coming off his fix. Yet, he needed to get away from this spot first, he told himself.

Before he could clear the sidewalk at the other end of the alley, however, police lights began flashing, and both ends of the alleyway were blocked by their cars. The teen turned to see whether the car that took the jewelry case had made its escape. But he couldn't tell.

He couldn't tell that all four men were undercover officers. He couldn't tell that he had been steered into this sting from the start. He couldn't tell that the original advice he got, or the original contact he was given—was to the police.

"You are being placed under arrest for trafficking in stolen jewelry and in drugs. You have the right to remain silent ..." one of the officers intoned as handcuffs were placed on the teen. A police officer in uniform again opened the jewelry case. It was all there—wait a minute, all but one necklace. The undercover crew congratulated each other on a tremendous bust.

***

Later that morning at the N.Y.U. campus, the sun was bright but not hot. During the time between classes, students hurried in various directions. Feury had taken a position on a bench near the front door for the film program. Because he had worked with Abdalla over the past while, he had come to know Abdalla's class life. With Feury's support, Abdalla no longer needed to sweep at McDonalds or open doors at the hotel. Instead, he was able to form a creative team with other students and collaborate with them, like he was doing when Feury spotted him.

"We will need to schedule time to talk about the script later," he said to a female student now on his creative team.

"Let me know what's going on. I only need to make some technical changes to the script. And I have a better idea as to how to end the film."

"Let's go with your idea."

"Thanks for your confidence. I want you to read it after I have finished."

"This all is so exciting. I'll talk to you later."

"I am also excited. I'm glad we are working together on this." With that comment, she walked down the steps, onto the sidewalk, and was absorbed into the crowd of students.

Feury stood up, signaled to Abdalla, and approached him. "How's your family? Any news?" he asked.

"My father is back with my family now. It looks like my oldest sister has a boyfriend."

"Well, that's all good news."

"Thanks for your help, Feury. I just wish that I could see them again. Really, I wish that they could see me here."

"They will," Feury said with resolve. "You worry about the film, and I'll worry about the family. By the way, how are things coming with the film?" Feury, as an investor, was always keen to assess how things were going and when, if needed, he should step in to give a hand in the guidance. He also was able to get stuck things unstuck.

"We did auditions today."

"Great. Say, are you graduating this year? Or do you have one more year before graduation?"

"I won't graduate until a year from now."

"So you have been here three years. And next year makes four."

"Yes, I cannot believe how long it has been since I last saw my mom, dad, and sisters. Just one more year."

"Speaking of your family, have you heard from your brother?"

"He came by my apartment a few weeks ago looking for money. I don't know what he is doing now."

"I haven't seen him, either. He's probably with some new gang."

"If my mother ever found out what he was doing here in America,…" Abdalla was lost in thought as he pictured, not an angry beating—that was not his parents' approach—but deep hurt as if something good had been taken away, like a family treasure such as a piece of land. The tie to ancestors would be weakened. "If my mother and father knew, they would be like plants pulled out by their roots."

"Why would that be the case?"

"Well, my parents taught us to follow the Lord and follow good biblical values. This country has too much temptation for him. Chijioke wants the easy life, not the life that comes from hard work and patience. He thinks only of himself, not of others who are equally down on their luck or in need of a hand."

"So, why didn't you mess up your life? You two are brothers and very close. You came from the same family in Africa; you settled in the same city—actually not far from each other. Why him and not you?"

Feury was really asking about himself. He had catered to people who wanted to escape or become rich and live a life of ease. Yet, he himself had never indulged such a fantasy. He served alcohol at his former club, but had not given himself free liquor drinks on the side. He had sold cigarettes and other stronger drugs, but had never desired such medications for himself.

Abdalla was also struck by the impact of this question. Why Chijioke, indeed? Somehow, he had thought that his brother had always taken the easy road. That seemed to be one factor. But another factor was that Chijioke never bothered to reflect on his course of action. How much better off was he after pursuing wealth?

To name one thing, Chijioke had sold off diamonds without talking to his dad and kept the money for himself. This action led to government intervention. Would Chijioke have stopped had he know that dad had also been harvesting and selling diamonds on the side?

Was what his father had done helpful? The money he got in illegal diamond sales made family life easier, but also unsustainable. As his mother had pointed out, eventually the diamonds would have been discovered by the government. How could this deeper struggle be reflected in his film?

He turned back to Feury and said, "I just kept at my school work and following the Lord. Things in this country—like the things in Africa—were not a temptation."

Sensing that he had triggered some soul searching in Abdalla and himself, Feury said, "You concentrate on the film, and I'll see what I can do to get your family here. I have to get papers for them all, and not everyone takes a bribe."

Abdalla knew that Feury was attempting to reassure him, but it had nearly the opposite effect. His family's freedom depended on many others like his brother taking money not due them. So could such corruption that usually leads to destruction also lead to good? So wasn't corruption alright sometimes?

"Feury, get papers for the boyfriend as well."

"Yes, even the boyfriend. Say, Abdalla, this might cheer you up. The hotel dropped the case against you. Just as you said, someone had stolen the jewels. A teenage boy as I understand it."

Abdalla's head swung up and his eyes brightened.

"He was a petty thief. But he attempted to sell the jewels to an undercover cop for drugs."

Another one seeking the pleasurable life. "Maybe God can turn his life around also?" Abdalla exclaimed.

CHAPTER

32

Both ends of the system needed to be worked and quickly so that the Ndaos—and an orphaned adult male—could depart from Senegal and be welcomed into the United States. The first end seemed straightforward as much as he could operate. Feury mailed Suma a letter. As she left the post office with this letter, opened it, and read it. She became so exciting that she jumped up and down. Could it be true that airplane tickets would be mailed to her for the entire family so that they could see Abdalla?

The second end was more complicated. Feury needed to work the connections from Senegal to New York. He went to a travel agent to book the tickets. Even though the price for four adults (he had to count them on his fingers: Issa and Suma, Sydney and Abimbola) and two younger daughters—that was six total tickets—was high, he had brought along enough cash to pay for the lot. The travel agent had not worked with one-thousand-dollar bills before and wasn't quite sure which president should be pictured on them. They had not been circulated since 1969, and even then when she had started working in travel, no one seemed to use them. So she had phoned her bank and been assured that Grover Cleveland was one of the two presidents on the 1928 green seal bills.

Suma needed to go to the U.S. embassy along with Issa and Sydney. Each family member and Sydney needed a visa so that they could emigrate and, hopefully, become citizens one day. The assistant to the assistant under-secretary, described how the floodgates had been opened for Africans to come to the U.S. In 1960 only 35,000 Africans had been given visas; in 1975 the Secretary of State expected this to more than double to over 80,000. The family was polite throughout the explanation, but were really only focused on their chances. These turned out to be excellent when one had a benefactor in the U.S. ready to vouch for support and care.

Admittedly, Feury's side was less daunting than Suma's. Her letter to him, confirming things to date, came on a tray while he was enjoying breakfast and reading his newspaper. When he finished breakfast and his reading, he opened the letter.

Meanwhile, Suma needed to stand in line at her post office. Finally, when it was her turn, she approached the clerk, who handed her a package. She had to sign for it, which she did, and carry it to a nearby counter. Inside, she found plane tickets for each person with his or her name on it. There at the bottom was a ticket for Sydney. Suma laughed when she saw this. Then she saw the dates on the tickets and knew that they all had much to do.

***

Feury leaned against a wall at the N.Y.U. campus with one foot firmly on the ground and the other one put against the wall. He knew when Abdalla's class ended and waited as the rush of students came out of the building. Then a small wash-back group walked up the steps into the building. Finally, as Feury had guessed, Abdalla walked out, talking with students on either side of him.

"I'll finish the editing tomorrow," one student said to Abdalla.

"The sound will be finished this afternoon," the other student said.

"That's great, guys," Abdalla said to both as he patted their backs.

Then the students grabbed their things and walked away. Seeing Feury, Abdalla walked directly to him. "What's up?"

"I have a surprise for you," Feury said.

"Oh yeah, I want to see it."

Feury held a pocket calendar in his hands, which he opened. "This is where we are," he said as he pointed to that day on the calendar. And then he flipped two months over, "And this is when your family is coming."

"Wait," Abdalla said, "my family is coming to America?"

"Yes."

"And this is the day they will be here?"

"Yes, as I tried to point out, it will be two months from this coming Saturday."

Abdalla shouted out loud, "Thank you, God. And thank you, Feury."

"But you know what this means?" Feury said as though a giant imposition were being placed on Abdalla. "It means that I've got to clean out my summer home on Staten Island to make room for your family."

"And the boyfriend?"

"Of course, the boyfriend. I don't want some forlorned young woman moping around my place crying or kicking furniture."

Abdalla gave Feury a big hug and said, "How thoughtful. Thanks *so* much. My family will be here for my graduation and the film's premier."

Then Abdalla continued jumping, until Feury said, "Okay, you can stop now."

***

Manhattan offered two sorts of soup kitchens the men who frequented the establishments had noted a long time ago. One they called "Jesus-soup" because the men had to line up, hear a reading, get an exhortation to let Christ live in them (or some such message), and pray to get serious or saved before they could eat.

The other they called by various names, but one common one was "germs" because the men had to line up, hear a reading, get an exhortation on the evils of reusing a needle or not washing, and practice washing their hands to get serious or be saved from infections and disease before they could eat.

The men, of course, used a different gauge. They compared the wait time before they could eat to the weight time—how much food got put on each tray? Well, that and the proximity of the soup kitchen to where they had been pan-handling before dinner time. In general, kitchens near the best tourist traffic areas—resident New Yorkers were not particularly given to making heart-felt contributions—that gave out the most food with the minimum of salvation (with Jesus or from germs) were the best.

Chijioke's measure was different still. He looked for compassionate, even friendly, staff as well as persons who would talk to him. On this day, he frequented one of his favorites. Of course, a long line had formed, but as he waited, he was able to talk with others near him in line. It made him feel human, even alive. While sitting on the sidewalk or sleeping in the park, most people pretended that he wasn't there— and, in a way, he wasn't. Out on the street, he existed as a hundred-sixty-pound black ghost who could only get people to walk off the sidewalk around him.

He drank, sure. But that was only to convert the coins people gave him into more invisible feeling time. Like pumping coins into a parking meter, drinking made him powerful enough to speed up time when he passed out. Putting himself in a stupor helped him get through the loss of all that money, all that fun, all that respect.

Now at the soup kitchen, God willing, he could see some familiar faces, get caught up on what's happening, and get some feeling back. It was his turn to walk through the line. He got his food, looked for a spot, and sat down—right next to a woman with her son. Although he was hungry, he didn't begin his meal until he had spoken with her son and then with her. Finally, he also bowed his head and prayed as his mother had taught him.

Oh, the simple things in life were the best, he thought to himself.

CHAPTER

33

Staten Island had only recent changed its name. It had been, until 1975, the Borough of Richmond. Located in the Southwest part of New York City—in one of its five boroughs brought together by bridges—it was close to New Jersey, but separated by the Arthur Kill and the Kill Van Kill. It was separated from Manhattan by the New York Bay. Yet, it attracted many New Yorkers to itself because, while it had the third largest amount land, it had the least amount of population. It was much more like a suburb.

The residences—houses situated on their properties—on Staten Island, then, tended to be large and expensive. Residents liked this for two reasons: on the one hand, it kept out those with only middle-class means; and, on the other hand, the extra space between residences made for good neighbors. Little wonder that, while Feury owned one, which he contemplated assigning to the Ndao family, he was shopping for a second.

"I can't believe how large and beautiful this place is, Feury," Abdalla exclaimed. "You may need to add servants to your roster to keep things at your current standards. I mean, I never thought that I would even go to a party in a place like this, much less know someone who owns such a property."

"Someday, Abdalla, you will live in a home like this. Just wait. I'm an extraordinary judge of talent."

***

The trip from Staten Island to John F. Kennedy Airport could be taken by subway, the ferry, or cabs. Feury asked Abdalla which option might be best for his family.

Abdalla was most familiar with the bus and subway system, especially in Manhattan and to or from John F. Kennedy Airport. He recognized, however, that this would involve several transfers—and with luggage and so many persons new to the underground mode of transportation, he ruled it out.

The Staten Island Ferry was maintained by the City of New York for one purpose: to get 20,000 persons each workday back and forth from Staten Island to Manhattan. Of course, it was crowded at the peak times in mornings and evenings, but there was no finer way to showcase the city with the Statute of Liberty and all the other features. The ride itself was fairly short at about 25 minutes. But, the image of getting to the ferry with all that luggage didn't appeal to either man.

As to cab, it could take nearly an hour when the traffic was favorable—and much longer when the traffic was not. Again, they would have eight persons coming back—Feury, Abdalla, Issa, Suma, the boyfriend, and three sisters. Again, the luggage could be an issue in loading it. But door-to-door service had its appeal. Feury suggested that they could simply split up into 3 groups and take an extra cab back. "Besides," he said, "you and I do not have luggage, Abdalla. This should give us extra space in one cab."

"Why are we trying to economize?" Feury asked. "Let's hire a van both ways from the limo service I usually use. It will have rows of seats for everyone as well as a place for all the luggage in the back—all the advantages of cabs, but we can all fit into one larger vehicle to continue our welcome and conversation."

Feury and Abdalla allowed plenty of time to make the trip, and they arrived early, especially in view of the fact that the passengers needed to clear customs and emigration.

Greeting arriving passengers at their gate was an attractive option for domestic travelers. For international passengers, in contrast, the meeting place was much closer to the loading-unloading zone. So the pair left their driver to wait with the limo while they went to the meeting place.

Watching passengers that emerged from the security process kept the two occupied with only a few side comments. They were amazed at the variety of persons flooding into the meeting area. Different persons with different ethic dress (with businessmen in white shirts, suits, and hats being the largest number) walked through the glass door-gates into the terminal lobby.

Finally, the Ndao family walked through the doors and into the terminal lobby. Suma rushed over to hug her eldest child. She burrowed her face and nose into his neck area—she couldn't reach his ears and temples. Then Issa came over to give his son a big bear hug, which nearly squeezed the breath from Abdalla's body. Then his sisters hugged him one after another, deeply and lovingly as though Abdalla had personally slayed the dragons and brought his family all to safety.

Feury watched from the side, thinking that he had already been repaid by what he had witnessed. Yet, he was anxious to hear the dialog among this family.

"You are finally here," Abdalla said to the entire family while looking mostly at his mother. I have missed you all and am glad to welcome you to my new world."

"We have also missed you so much," she replied as if speaking for the entire family.

"Son, who is the person responsible for making this happen?"

Abdalla stepped forward and made a circling motion when he said, "Everyone," and then turned and gestured with his open arms toward someone standing in the background, "this is Feury Seger." Then Abdalla stepped backward to bring Feury into the family circle.

Issa was the first to step forward, and he grabbed Feury's hand to shake and shake it while he said, "Thank you so much for all you have done for Abdalla and this family."

"It's a pleasure to meet you," Feury said, his voice a bit shaky as Issa continued to pump his hand.

"We owe you a debt of gratitude," Suma said as she stepped forward to give him a huge hug. "Thank you so much for your generosity."

"Yes," Issa continued, "thank you so much for getting us here. I cannot imagine all the contacts and paperwork needed to make this come true."

"No problem," Feury said sincerely, while becoming self-conscious at all the accolades.

Sensing this, Abdalla stepped forward again to ask, "Now, where is that boyfriend?"

A young man stepped forward, and Abdalla scanned him from head to toe. He wanted to size up this young man, not knowing how exactly to approach a would-be lover of his younger sister. The young man's hair was trimmed short, like a military cut. His eyes were steady, and Sydney peered into Abdalla's eyes and Abdalla looked into his. As their hands touched, Abdalla observed the young man's strong muscular physique. His waist was trim. The young man's grip was firm. Abdalla liked what he saw in his sister's man.

Then Suma clutched her hands and moved them near to her cheekbone. Her smile was wide with dimples showing. "Feury, you were the financial means, and God was the force behind you!"

This caught Feury off guard. He was a pious man, but not deeply religious—not seeing God's hand behind favorable outcomes, especially ones where he wrote the check. "Well, that's up for discussion," he said while bowing a bit.

Abdalla had forgotten how transparent his mother was about her faith and her interpretation of events. Somehow, he might need to contain his mother's enthusiasm in the moment for a later time when these things could be discussed.

"Feury, you don't believe in God?" Abdalla heard her ask.

"Hmm. Not really."

Abdalla attempted to step between them, but his mother quickly moved around him, her eyes focused on Feury, like a hunter's gaze on a target for dinner.

"What happened to us in Africa was a horrible thing," she began in a serious tone. "But God was in control of it all. It was very hard to suffer for several years, but God was getting us ready to come here. If we did not let go of our home and our homeland, we would have missed God's greatest blessing…"

Two porters had pushed flat-bed carts piled high with suitcases near their circle, and an airport security guard arrived behind them. "Look, folks, you're gonna hafta move otta the way. You're blocking the lobby. More people need to come thru this way."

Feury smiled at Suma and politely said, "Welcome to New York."

Everyone laughed, grabbed a hand, and walked toward the limo.

***

Feury had plenty of footsteps to rethink his transportation plan. Suma held his hand tightly, and he feared that she would not let go until he had professed belief in God's guiding hand. And the seating arrangement didn't help matters. He sat next to Suma, while Issa and Abdalla shared a seat. Then Abimbola and Sydney shared a seat. And finally the other two girls in the last seat. The porters and driver had stuffed the luggage into the back area and in the front rider's seat. The vehicle was so full that it seemed like the entire family was present.

Feury had opened the door for Suma, but when the conversation began, she turned to the seat behind her to ask Abdalla, "So how is Chijioke?"

"I don't quite know, mom. He got a girl pregnant, then he stayed with me for a while. Then he left, and I have not heard from him since."

"Oh, no," she gasped. She had missed having all her family together at the airport, but she hadn't anticipated that Chijioke would be in trouble.

"Last I knew, he was homeless."

"Well, I pray to God that he is safe."

"We all do," Feury said while he touched Suma's hand.

CHAPTER

34

The daytime for Chijioke was the hardest, the time after the shelter dismissed the men from the beds used the night before, but before the evening homeless meal. The daytime provided nothing but, well, time—and competition for the best spots to guilt tourists into tossing spare change into a cup.

Chijioke had not been able to keep his suits or ties. Yet, he had kept that sense of class, that flair for dressing just so. He converted some of the contributions he received into food, McDonald's mostly. And he purchased liquor on occasion, but not the rot-gut stuff. He tried to save his money, but usually spent or gave to others whatever he got that day.

Today, the offerings he had received amounted to nearly fifteen dollars. In his former life, that was tip money for a waitress who has been kind or attentive. Now it was a good day's take. And he had in mind just to whom he would give some of it.

As he walked toward his favorite dinner spot, two tall, beefy men began to follow him. He didn't notice at first, until he heard their shoes stomp the sidewalk and then he saw their reflections in a store window. He picked up his pace; they speeded up as well. He started to run, and they did as well. Then each burly man grabbed one of Chijioke's arms, lifted him up off the sidewalk, and carried him into an alleyway with his shoes in the air still attempting to get away.

They didn't say anything to him. They set him down on the concrete. One held him while the other hit him in the face. Chijioke reached into his pocket to proffer the change. But the men exchanged places, and the other man slugged him in the gut. Chijioke went down on the ground, his head throbbing and his gut exploding from poor nutrition and rich amounts of drinking. The men repeated this pattern, each taking his turn. Then they ran away as though they had challenged each other to touch or sock a dead body.

As Chijioke lay in the alleyway, he thought about the other time he had been in that alley—in the dumpster, in fact. He tried to sniff, but his nose was bloodied. He couldn't smell anything or even taste the blood in his throat. He planned to wait to get up until the men were gone…but he fell unconscious.

When he awoke, he listened for the noise of shoes or heavy breathing, in case the two men were still nearby. Chijioke ached too much to try to get up. His eye was swelling shut as the tears from that eye backed up into its socket. He had never felt so alone, so disconnected from life, so in his body and out of it at once. If he could have cried out for help, it would have been to his mother. Knowing she could not rescue him, he closed his eyes and drifted away.

CHAPTER

35

The van pulled into the driveway, and then pulled right into a large parking area near the entrance. It was a two-story house, surrounded by wrought-iron fencing, but oriented to take advantage of the ocean view. The façade gave the impression of three sections: the center had rough stone of yellows and whites mortared into place. On either side were back plastered walls painted in a golden color. The door was a deep red. Issa recognized it instantly as the same colors as his family colors.

At Feury's guidance, the family walked to the center section, up the steps, and through the door. There in the foyer, Issa looked up to see the entry rise up over two stories with a chandler attached far above. The floor was a white marble and the walls were a white with dark wood trim. An archway to the right opened into a living room whose ceiling again went up two stories. It had a fireplace and mantle, couches and chairs, great for hosting receptions or entertaining. With almost 8,000 square feet of space, the nine bedrooms and eleven bathrooms (not counting the finished basement or the servant's quarters) were each spacious. Of course, they had not seen the lagoon-style in-ground pool or its patio or any of the other amenities.

"This is a fancy hotel," Issa said to Abdalla.

"No, father, this is not a hotel. It will be your home now."

Meanwhile, almost straight ahead from the entrance was a stairway to the second floor. The girls had already scampered up the stairs. Feury was close behind them, sharing in their utter joy at being in such a home.

"Girls, this is your home now," he said. "There is a bedroom for each of you. Go find one you like, but don't take your parent's bedroom."

Abimbola, Amia, and Aba toured the rooms as a group as they screamed upon entering each room. Feury went back downstairs to welcome the rest of the family.

"This home is bigger than anything I've ever seen," Issa exclaimed.

"This is small compared to what is really out there," Feury replied modestly.

"Small?"

"Dad, Feury is right. This is nothing to what is out there."

"Feury, do you own this house?" Suma asked.

"Yes, for right now. But eventually Abdalla will own it."

"How do you pay for something like this?" she continued.

"I knew you would ask a question like that. Abdalla's film will pay for it. When he becomes well-known in the film industry, he will pay for it himself."

Suma and Issa looked at each other with widening eyes.

"Oh, yes," Suma continued, "we need to hear more about your big-selling film."

"I will be happy to share more about it later. Now we need to get you all unpacked and settled into your new home and homeland."

Then Abdalla turned to Feury. "Thanks so much for all that you have done for me and my family."

"It's not a problem, Abdalla. I'm just glad to participate in your success."

"Now, all we need is Chijioke," Suma sighed.

"I'm working on that, too," Feury assured her.

***

Chijioke woke up again still lying in the alley way. At first he didn't recognize where he was. His head hurt as though he was coming out of a bender, but he couldn't remember drinking anything recently. No, the last thing he could remember was being slugged repeatedly by two large men. That's right, he confirmed in his mind as his body's pains began to register. His left eye was swollen shut. He had a cut on his upper lip. And his stomach felt like it had been pounded against his spine.

Had he needed the sleep or was he unconscious? Two nights ago, he recalled, one man in the homeless shelter had snored so loud that Chijioke could not sleep. Yesterday, he recalled sitting in the park—the day was warm with little breeze and blue skies. He remembered waking up from a nap under an oak tree in the park. So here, he must have been unconscious.

Had he really been punched that hard in the stomach or had he not been eating? Bright brown eyes came to his mind. The children had bright brown eyes. He had been at the soup kitchen last night. The soup was awful, not just watery or offering a burnt taste, but had the aroma of old shoes, or so he imagined. A family sat next to him, and the children ate the food without complaint. Perhaps they didn't know what fine food tasted like, he thought. No, at some time, they must have had at least one good meal. No, they ate because that is what their parents said they needed to do before they could go play with others. They had finished their meal, swinging their legs, ready to go. Well, he had eaten, so he had been punched that hard.

As Chijioke continued these thoughts in order to reconnect his mind and body, a sound rang down the alleyway.

"Chijioke, is that you?"

It was a man's voice. Chijioke thought that the men had come back to accost him again. So he stirred, desperately trying to get up, stand on his feet, and run away. But all he could do was roll from lying on his stomach to lying on his back. Then he propped himself up with his elbows.

"Hey, Chijioke!" the voice called again.

"What do you want, man?" Chijioke replied.

"Get in the car."

"I'm not getting into a car."

"Feury Seger wants to see you."

"Sorry, but I don't want to see him."

"He needs to see you."

"For what?"

"He sent us to find you. He said he has something for you."

As Chijioke's eyes focused, he recognized the men in the car as part of Feury's former crew of bouncers and thugs. He slowly got up, put out his arms and hands like a high-wire walker until he could regain his balance, and stepped like a man tip-toeing through a sobriety test. The two men roared with disgust.

Then one opened his door, got out, opened the back door, and make some adjustments. When he turned to help Chijioke get in, Chijioke saw that he had carefully positioned a clean old blanket. The man had tucked it behind a head-rest, stuffed a row of it tightly where the back and seat cushions met, and then allowed the rest of the blanket to flow over the seat cushion's front edge and toward the floorboard.

Chijioke put his left hand on the blanketed seat-back to steady himself, but this pulled some of the blanket out at the top. He put his right hand on the front passenger's headrest, put his left foot on the floorboard, and swung himself in.

"Hey, watch where you put your hands and body," the man said while he put his hands under Chijioke's arms to help him land on the blanket. Once in, the man closed the door and got back into his front rider's seat. The driver started the engine, flipped the air conditioning to high, and then revved the engine in hopes of hurrying the flow of cool, fresh air.

"Where are we going?"

The driver turned to his accomplice and said, "To see your mother."

"What?" Chijioke asked, because the engine and fan created too much noise.

The driver pulled the shift into drive, stepped on the gas pedal, and guided the car back onto the street and through traffic. Chijioke decided to let the ride happen; it could be no worse than the beating he had taken. And if they shot him? Well, that might be all right. He loathed his current life, even when he felt powerless to change it. He had always sought the easy way out, and maybe death now could be that option.

With the traffic only moderate, the drive from Manhattan to Staten Island took a little over an hour. Once they reached the Island, the properties became expansive and posh. Chijioke thought that he might have purchased a property for his family in this neighborhood—if his money had grown, or at least lasted.

Not far from the ocean, the car pulled into a driveway and turned to the right into a parking area. The driver stopped and then turned to Chijioke. "Get out! Now!"

The command was so forceful that Chijioke had pulled the handle to open his door as a reflex. "Where are we?" he asked. In his current condition, he didn't want to be dumped into a privileged neighborhood where he could find no services, no help.

The man in the passenger's seat turned around and put a gun in Chijioke's face. "The man said, 'Get out, now'! So get out!"

Chijioke swung his door open and slowly got out of his seat. He pushed the door shut, while the passenger rolled down his window. "You've got a surprise waiting," he mocked. Then both men laughed as they had at the start of the journey.

The driver sounded his horn twice, backed up, and exited out the driveway, while Chijioke stood there and watched his ride escape from this spot.

***

After a few moments, Chijioke's judgment of time no longer keen, he decided to get it over with. He slowly stepped to the front door, rang the door bell, and waited.

Feury opened the door. "Well, well, who do we have here? Chijioke, come inside."

Chijioke looked down at his baggy pants and misfit shoes. He was suddenly embarrassed at how he looked and smelled. He began brushing each sleeve off with a hand and then rubbed the front of his shirt.

"The guys in the car said you wanted to see me," Chijioke said while pointing over his shoulder toward the parking lot.

"Yes, I did. I wanted you to meet some people," Feury said as Suma and Issa came around the corner.

Still standing outside, Chijioke called through the doorway into the foyer, "Mom, dad," as he continued to wipe his shoes on a doormat.

His parents froze at what they saw. Their mouths dropped and their countenance shifted from joy to anger. "Hello, son," Issa said in an icy tone.

"Hi, dad; hi, mom," Chijioke said in a hesitant voice.

"Oh, what have you been doing with yourself?" his mother asked.

"You look, son, like a bum," his father offered.

"Oh, ah, I've been around."

"It looks like it," Feury said in an attempt to bring some humor to this awkward meeting. But no one laughed.

"Is this what we taught you, son?" his mother asked.

"You look like you've not eaten in a while."

If this was a shift to some conversation, it failed.

Issa continued, "Your brother tells us that you have been into gangs, been sleeping around with women, and doing drugs."

Chijioke had no more politeness from which to draw. He felt punched again in the stomach now by his brother.

In spite of their knowledge and disgust, Suma and Issa moved toward the doorway to get closer to their son…until they caught wind of him. Chijioke stunk of urine and garbage. His teeth were stained from red wine and no maintenance.

Suma waved her hand in front of her nose in hopes of pushing away the fowl air and bringing closer some fresh air. "When was the last time you bathed?" she asked.

"Obviously, not for a while," Issa joined in. "Do you realize what you put your family through?"

"No, not really," Chijioke replied, recalling what he had been through.

So much anger washed over Issa that he could no longer put his feelings into words. He threw a punch at his son, but Chijioke who had just been through a beating lifted his arms to fend off the blows. Issa grabbed Chijioke and spun him around, throwing him to the floor. Then Issa jumped on top of him and this time landed punched after punch. Legs akimbo kicked an umbrella stand to the floor. Then Chijioke got up, but Issa tackled him, and they crashed into a table opposite the doorway, sending it skittering across the floor.

When Abdalla, Sydney, and the girls heard the noises, they rushed to the banister to see what could be going on. Aba turned to Abdalla and said, "Chijioke is in big trouble with mom and dad. Right?"

"Yes, he is in big trouble."

Using the handrail, Abdalla headed down the stairs.

Meanwhile, Chijioke had managed to get free again and was in a stand-off with his father. On the sidelines, his mother again entered the fray. "Look at you, son. What a stinking mess."

"Are you really living on the streets? What good does that bring to your life?" his father asked.

"Do you realize that what you did in Africa—your own selfish actions—caused the girls not to go to school and us to starve?" Suma asked while pointing a finger at him.

"Maybe he doesn't care!" Issa concluded.

"I'm really sorry, mom and dad, but I don't care."

Chijioke tried to slow the bleeding from his upper lip, where he had been hit by one of the two men earlier.

With such an uncaring reply, Issa again attacked Chijioke and again brought him to the floor with punches. Suma, Abdalla, and Feury worked as hard as they could to separate the two men.

"Issa, stop hitting him," Suma cried.

"Didn't-we-teach-you-anything?" Issa said with each word marking a blow to Chijioke.

Finally, Chijioke got free of Issa's grip and ran out the doorway. No one ran after him to get him to come back.

CHAPTER
36

The registrar's office was an academic courtroom of sorts. Applicants came with their dreams and transcripts in hopes of being admitted to the college. Students, whose work was not to the college's standards, often came to drop a course by the drop-date or appeal for a change-of-grade if they had missed the deadline. Finally, graduates often came to the registrar's office to have certified transcripts sent to graduate schools or first-job interviews.

What made this registrar so pleasing to students and faculty alike was her attempt at balanced judgments in which new applicants could find the best fit, find alternatives that held students accountable for learning, and still kept up with all the paperwork so that transcripts could be mailed quickly.

Aba and Amia sat in the two chairs the registrar's office provided. Behind them Abimbola and Sydney stood, holding hands. Paper was stacked in three neat piles on the registrar's desk. Everything the registrar did was filled out in triplicate. The original was filed in the student's master file; the yellow copy was filed by sequence number off campus for backup; and the pink copy went to accounting so that student's tuition and fees could be adjusted as needed. Behind her were shelves of books from floor to ceiling with titles about management, best practices, issues in student counseling, and the like.

No doubt, the day of reckoning was at hand for the four young adults. Even though they were quite sure they would receive fair treatment, each student was more than a bit anxious about her or his outcome.

The registrar sat in her chair and began, "I think you will find this school to be exactly what you all need. We are highly recommended and accredited." She paused to look into the eyes of each person, then she turned back to the paperwork in front of her. "Abimbola, Aba, and Amia, I see here from your records and letters of recommendation from the school director in Africa that you all did very well."

"We were A students according to American standards," Amia assured her.

"Then, it looks like you all had a lapse in your education. Can you tell me more about this?"

"We fell on hard times," Abimbola said somewhat embarrassed, even though she had not caused the lapse.

"I'm sorry to hear that. And how did you come to learn English?"

"Missionaries came to our country and taught us how to speak, read, and write English," Aba replied.

"Knowing that you three did well in school and are well versed in English, especially reading and writing, you should have no problem attending the school. We will need to do some placement testing to see where you all are at in our core requirements and at what level." The registrar leaned on her elbows and clasped her hands together as she said this.

"That is good. Thank you," Amia said.

"Sydney, I'm afraid you will need to be in a different class because you do not read or write English to our standards."

"I understand," he replied.

***

Life on Staten Island proceeded as though the incident with Chijioke had not occurred. That was only one of the pretenses, however. The other pretense was that Feury somehow gave or provided for the Ndao family the means by which to relocate in America. In fact, the costs for getting Issa released from jail, emigration papers from the African government, travel expenses, and this huge home— a new film director's anticipated huge success bankrolled the entire operation.

A few mornings later, Suma, Issa, Abdalla, and Feury were by the pool having breakfast served to them. Instead of scrambled eggs and toast, however, the servants had made an effort to cook with more influences from Africa. This meant more fruit and vegetables as well as smaller amounts of meat proteins.

"Feury, how can we ever thank you for helping us?" Suma asked.

"When the film does well, then you can pay me back."

"What are Abdalla's plans today?" Issa wanted to know.

"He had to go to school to do some last minute editing on the film," Feury replied. "He has to get the film ready for the Film Festival next week. He has worked very hard on this film."

"We taught our children to work hard," Issa said with pride.

"We also taught our children to have faith in God," Suma added.

"God must not be very kind to let you go through what you went through."

"But if we did not go through the hard times, we never would have let go of what we want; we never would have let God do what God wanted, which was to bring us here. That is what trust in God is all about," Suma said.

Issa added, "I was really angry for losing my land that was in my family for centuries. But God had different plans for us. I never would have thought I would be living in the United States."

"It was very hard struggling, but God had our lives in his hands. Everything was in his control," Suma assured.

"Feury, I would never call myself a religious man, but God provided for us in miraculous ways."

"And God was with us through all the dangers and distresses."

"Wait," Feury interrupted the pair. "God let you lose your home and land, but God was with you and provided for you?"

He paused for a moment. Suma was about to speak, but Feury signaled that he wanted to say more.

"So God rips the hammock from underneath you and then catches you on your way down?"

"Yes," Issa said. "That is how it feels."

"God is good, all the time," Suma added.

"How can God be good when he is turning your hammock upside down?" Feury asked.

"Can we expect only good times and not bad times?" Suma countered.

"So we should expect both?" Feury asked.

"Trials make us stronger by giving us endurance and character."

"Ahh. How is that again?"

Suma slowed down as though she were speaking to a child.

"The trial, pain, or suffering helps you grow. It is like a catapult to bring you into maturity. But trials can also make you bitter, if you let them."

"So an easy life isn't promised?"

"True, but God's presence is. When you go through the difficulty, God is there to encourage and strengthen you."

"A presence that reassures, but may not rescue you. I will have to think about this," Feury said.

***

Cutting out extraneous materials, while keeping a story rich with sub-plots and twists—that was the final, and most important, job of a director. Abdalla thought of artists as doing one of two activities: for visual artists and writers, they begin with a blank canvas or sheet of paper, which they need to fill in; but for sculptors and film directors, they start with a full block of stone or a full screen, which they need to pare back the excess material in order to leave the right proportion as a three-dimensional object or a storyline without any clutter or distraction.

For Abdalla, this meant editing the film so that the viewer has enough context all the time to follow the story. But the problem for all directors, especially new ones, was this: the director has pictured the scene so many times that it can make sense to the director, but not to the first-time viewer. So Abdalla had engaged a student who had not previously worked on the film in order not to make a beginner's mistake. Abdalla would spend most of his time on this tightening process until the festival.

CHAPTER

37

A squirrel left to its own devises organizes and manages its food supply. But if that squirrel is moved to another location, it can encounter unforeseen danger or not find enough food quickly.

Being homeless was something like this. Chijioke in Staten Island could have withered within a few days. By going back to his several blocks of Manhattan, however, he could survive indefinitely. Now that he could see out of both eyes again, his lip was back to normal, and his ribs were no longer ached when he walk—he was ready to survive on his terms.

As he walked north on Madison Avenue, the aroma of fresh bread filled his nose. Up ahead was one of his favorite bakeries, and he could taste the bread, so warm and filling. As he approached, he passed an alleyway and decided to check there first. Inside in wax-lined boxes, he saw large loaves of bread. He pulled one out of the box and was about to eat it, when the back door to the bakery opened. A baker had another two boxes.

"Excuse me," Chijioke asked, "but are you throwing away this bread?"

"Yeah, it's too old to sell. But, if you are hungry, then take as much as you want."

"Thank you, sir. You are so kind."

"Hey, good luck with everything," the baker said. "I hope you can get back on your feet."

"Me, too."

Chijioke carefully stacked the three boxes one on top of the other and carefully he walked down the street.

***

Each spring, the Kanbar Institute of Film and Television presented the First Run Festival to showcase over 120 advanced projects in film, video, and animation. The New York University Tisch School of the Arts on Broadway hosted the film portion. Undergraduate advanced production videos could run no longer the 30 minutes. Before Christmas the previous year, Abdalla had submitted a short and a script to the panel that judged submissions. Only a few proposals were accepted each year, and Abdalla's was one of those. Since Christmas, he and his crew of students had been shooting film, assembling the takes, and editing. Now came the test of his abilities.

People filled the auditorium, talking or sharing notes on the festival. Near the front, Abdalla and his guests were seated together. On the far right was Issa and Suma and next to them were the missionary from New York (and Abdalla's landlord for the past four years), Pastor John and his wife. On the other side, next to Abdalla, sat Feury. Like the rest of the audience, they talked and enjoyed the anticipation before the opening.

Then the announcer approached the microphone.

"Tonight, we are introducing another film from a student here at NYU. He lived in Africa all his life before coming to the United States to pursue a degree in film. That has been his dream since he was very young. He is also here with his family who just arrived from Africa, and they are planning to stay and become citizens."

The crowd clapped and cheered loudly.

"This student was awarded a full scholarship to his program and has done extremely well in school. I would like to introduce him now. He is Abdalla Ndao. Let's give him a nice round of applause."

The crowd cheered loudly as Abdalla got up to the microphone to speak.

"Thank you all for coming. Of course, some of you have been in this film, so you know what it is about. For those of you who don't, it is about my life in America. It has been good coming to America. I love this country."

Everyone cheered louder than before. Across the crowd, many took up the chant, 'U.S.A.,' 'U.S.A.,' Abdalla waited smiling for the cheering to subside. Then he continued:

"I just want to say thank you to all of you who helped with the film. I want to thank my producer, Feury Seger, my family, and especially my mom and dad. And, of course, I would like to thank Almighty God for getting me here to fulfill my dreams of directing movies. I have been here in the country only four years now and…"

Everyone again clapped and cheered.

"...and I have had some experiences living here. Of course, it has been through a student's eyes for this film. Maybe getting into the real world, things will look quite different."

Abdalla and the crowd chuckled at "student eyes" versus "real world."

"Thanks to my friends, students, and professors here at NYU for their dedication and vision to help me with this film. I would like to thank Mary Pollock for her help in writing my screenplay, Jeff Murdock for his help with sound, and Germaine Clark for his camera work. This was a collaborative effort."

Again the crowd clapped and cheered, and for the first time, Abdalla understood they wanted to get to the film. So he decided to shorten his introduction.

"Most of you live in the U.S. so I think it will be interesting to see how a foreigner views your country. I hope you like it. So sit back and enjoy the film."

Again everyone clapped, and Abdalla sat down. The lights dimmed, the curtain opened to expose the large screen. As he was seated, he saw his mother signal how proud she was of his accomplishments. And the film began.

CHAPTER

38

Chijioke was walking the street again. He did not feel well, and he certainly did not look well. His cheeks were puffy, his belly was slightly bloated, and his stomach was upset. He felt the urge to vomit and got close enough to a garbage can to spew the container with the vile things he had been eating lately. He hurt so much that he began to cry. Sleep, he thought, maybe he needed to rest a bit. So he found the side of a building that hid him from plain sight. He laid down and fell asleep.

Later, when he awoke, the evening was approaching, and he was hungry again. He wondered if the bakery might again have some old bread. He walked there and found some bread in the dumpster. But this bread had been in there a while. The bottom crust had mold, and bugs had found it before Chijioke. Yet, he was so hungry that he shook off the bugs and wiped off the mold he saw. People who passed by saw him picking off the last bugs, and they became disgusted. But he didn't care; he was hungry.

Hoping to get at the freshest part of a loaf, Chijioke broke one loaf in half. He caught a whiff of the bread when it had been fresher. And the smell and action of breaking it in two made him think about the Lord's Supper back in his Christian church:

"Broken for you, for the forgiveness of your sins."

His eyes blinked for a moment. Then, when he bit into the inner part of the loaf, the words his mother taught came ringing:

"...give us this day our daily bread and forgive us our sins as we forgiven those who sin against us..."

He began to sob.

"I am so sorry for my selfish living. I have only thought of myself."

And those who passed him by sobbing in the alley had pity on him.

That same evening, Abdalla was in line at graduation for his degree. Sorted alphabetically by last name, the line stretched out before him and behind him. Finally, Abdalla was next. He waited in the box, his name was called, he approached the podium to receive his degree, shook the hand of the man handing out the scrolls, flipped his tassel from one said to the other, and then walked to the other side of the dais and down the steps. His undergraduate days were finished.

***

When Chijioke awoke that night, he was still tucked in by the building. He was safe. He walked back to the bakery alleyway and sat in front of the dumpster. The words welled up inside of him:

"Heavenly Father, I am so sorry for messing up my life. I really need your help. Please God I am tired of living like this. I want to go home. Take me home, Lord."

Then he slid himself close to the building by the dumpster, laid his head back, and fell asleep again.

The next morning, Chijioke hit the street in search of another source of food. At first, he didn't notice that a car was following him, the men inside watching him. Then he spotted the car with the two men who had taken him to Staten Island. He recalled that trip as being not so pleasant—or easy for him to get back to his neighborhood. As he debated whether to run, the passenger rolled down his window and called out, "Chijioke!"

He eyed the man.

"What do you guys want now?"

"Your mommy wants to see you."

The passenger said this in a taunting manner.

"Yeah, well is my father going to beat me again?"

"Just get in."

Chijioke opened the rear passenger door, saw the blanket already set up, and got into the car and sat in his place.

Then he noticed a gym bag. To avoid a repeat of the previous trip, the men took Chijioke to the Harlem YMCA on 135th Street to scrub his head and body, and to put on some different clothes.

***

When the car arrived at the Staten Island home, Chijioke could hear the party in the back. Puffs of smoke curled their way through the parking area along with the aroma of meat grilling. This time the car didn't use a horn signal or drive off quickly. Instead, the driver and passenger got out of the car with Chijioke, and they walked slowly to the front door. Even though he smelled better and looked much better, Chijioke didn't feel better.

When the driver rang the bell, Feury opened the door and invited them in. Chijioke peered into the foyer, looking first to the right and then to the left. Seeing no one else, he stepped into the home. Then the other two quickly followed into the foyer.

"Hey you guys, how about something to eat. We have hot dogs, hamburgers, and steaks," Feury told them.

"And chicken!"

Aba added this as she joined the parade to the patio area around the pool.

The two men went over to the grill. Chijioke lingered with Feury.

"Chijioke, what will you have?"

He didn't respond.

"Buddy, I hate to say it, but in spite of your cleanup, you look terrible."

"Is anyone going to fight with me today?"

"No. Today is a happy occasion."

"What are we celebrating?"

"One, your sisters are back in school. Two, Abimbola has a boyfriend. Three, your brother finished school; he has a degree. And four, he is pursuing his film project with me—a feature film."

"Wow. That's a lot."

"So what do you want to eat?"

"I'll have a hamburger," Chijioke said, licking his lips.

"Well, here it is, hot off the grill. The fixings are over on that table," Feury said as he handed Chijioke a hamburger.

Then Chijioke headed for the condiment table.

"Hello, little brother," Abdalla said as he walked up beside Chijioke.

"Hi, Abdalla. Sorry I missed your film festival and graduation, but I didn't know."

"That's alright, Chijioke. We're brothers, right?" Abdalla said as the two brothers hugged each other.

"Thank you for being such a faithful brother."

Then his mother came over to the table, and she hugged Chijioke. He lingered in her arms, feeling her reassuring grasp. Suma had tears in her eyes, and she could not say anything. She simply mouthed the words, I love you.

Then after a few minutes, she said, "Hello, son. How are you doing?"

"Not so well, mom. I think I'm really sick."

She stepped back. "Oh, my. You don't look well at all. Why don't you stay here, and we can take care of you? Your family really cares about you."

"Sorry, mom, but dad doesn't care about me."

"Oh yes he does. He was just angry. But he's gotten over that."

"Well," Chijioke confessed, "I'm so sorry for what I have done to this family and to myself."

"We forgive you, Chijioke, and so does God."

"If I had only known what would happen to all of you, I would never have sold those diamonds."

"Chijioke, listen to me. What you did not know was that your father was already selling the diamonds he was finding so that he could provide for us and so that you all could go to school. I am sure this might have happened at some point. But the diamond dealer your father was selling the diamonds to was a reputable man. He really cared for us as a family and worked to protect us."

"I did not know that."

"Chijioke, always remember: When God takes something away from us, he always gives us something better in return. Or God will give it back later, better than before."

"Mom, I'm so glad to talk with you again. But I really don't feel well."

"Then, let's take you to a doctor right away."

"I'm hungry, but I cannot eat this burger, mom. I really need help."

"I know. Let's go now."

CHAPTER

39

The hospital room was white with a faint smell of disinfectant. Chijioke lay in the bed sleeping, with an I.V. in one arm and an oxygen mask over his nose and mouth. He had a heart monitor attached to his other arm, and except for this machine's steady beeps, the room was quiet. A doctor went into his room, examined the patient, and recorded current information in the patient's chart at the end of the bed.

Suma, Issa, and Abdalla were all in the family waiting area. When Suma saw the doctor go into Chijioke's room, she quickly moved to the doorway and waited for the doctor to exit.

When he stepped out, she asked, "How is our son?"

"He came into the hospital with a rare situation I haven't seen since my residency in Africa. Your son had a low-grade malaria coupled with severe malnutrition. Had we not treated the malaria, we would not have been able to overcome his serious malnutrition."

"But I thought that malaria would be fatal within a year if it were not treated. How can he have had this for such a long time?" Suma asked.

"Well, *Plasmodium falciparum* is the most severe and life-threatening form of the disease. But there are three other forms, and your son has *Plasmodium vivax*. This is much less deadly on its own, but it can be aggravated by severe malnutrition."

"And what part of Africa did you do your residency?"

"Senegal. Why?"

"That is where we are from."

"Wow, what a coincidence," the doctor replied. "So what are you doing in the states?"

"We live here now."

"Well, that's great. Welcome, and I'm glad I was here to recognize this condition or your son could have been close to death for days...maybe even died. But now he should be able to go home in a few days; he is in good hands."

"Yes, he is," Suma agreed.

After the doctor left, Suma told the others about the conversation.

Abdalla said, "That was no coincidence that this doctor was prepared to identify a condition from our homeland."

"God is watching over Chijioke and us."

"Yes, God is indeed watching over all of us," Issa agreed.

Issa and Suma held hands as the group left the hospital.

***

A few days later, Chijioke was on the back patio, sitting in a chair in his bathrobe. Even though he was out of the hospital, he was still restricted as to what he could eat. But soup was on the menu, and he was enjoying a large bowl of it with his parents.

As he finished, he heard noises behind him from the hallway back to the home's foyer. A young woman appeared and Suma, who saw her first, motioned her to come over.

"Hi, my name is Suma."

"I'm Tyesha. And this is…"

Chijioke's head turned. He hadn't heard that voice in maybe three years. She looked as stunning as she had when he first met her. "Hey, baby."

"Hi, Chijioke. How are you feeling? Your brother told me you were in the hospital."

"I'm feeling much better. I got out a few days ago."

A little face peeked out from behind Tyesha's skirt.

"Who is this little girl?" Chijioke said to a shy but striking child.

"I want you to meet your daughter, Angela," Tyesha said.

"She is so cute," he said, while make a big smiley face for her.

"Well, she looks like her father."

"Tyesha, I want to be a better man. I've been thinking ever since I got out of the hospital."

"Thinking about what?"

"About you and me. I'm sorry I rejected you. I have been so incredibly selfish. It's been all about my comfort."

"I've been thinking about you, too," she said.

"I've had plenty of time to begin reading my Bible again and to get back to God."

Tyesha smiled. "That's an answer to my prayers."

"I never stopped loving you."

"And I never stopped loving you, mister high-roller come low."

"I want to make a commitment to you to never leave you and to always love you."

Tyesha began to cry as Chijioke lifted and opened his arm, beckoning her to give him a hug.

"I love you, too," she said as she bent down to hug him—and give him a kiss on the cheek.

"I only want to be with you. Now, can I hold Angela?"

CHAPTER

40

The Tyesha and Chijioke wedding was a mid-summer event at the Staten Island home on the lawn; for the reception, the party moved adjacent to the patio and pool. Tyesha had worn a white wedding gown with a modest neckline and a more open back. The skirt just reached the floor, giving her mobility for catching Angela.

Aba, Abimbola, and Amia wore matching bridesmaid's dresses all in a powder blue. Chijioke wore a black tuxedo, and his groomsmen—Abdalla, Feury, and Sydney—wore powder blue tuxedoes (not their favorite color). Angela was dressed as a flower girl, but she got more interested in petals that had already fallen on the aisle runner than on sprinkling them along the way.

The dinner event was spectacular. After the meal, Suma and Issa sat with Feury.

"Could you have imagined it? Just eight months ago, things were completely different," Suma said as she was picturing all the changes.

"We were homeless in Africa," Issa said. "And I was jailed several times."

"Abdalla finished school and now has an award-winning film to show around for director jobs."

"The girls are in school again," Issa noted.

"Chijioke was in the hospital with a condition that could have taken his life."

"Abimbola has a boyfriend," Issa said, "and lets hope that relationship moves slowly."

"You moved to the states," Feury added.

"My, so much has changed. God has been good," Suma concluded.

"Yes we have been through a lot, and God has been good," Issa agreed.

***

You attend films, but you haven't heard of me, Abdalla Ndao?

That's probably because I haven't made it big enough yet. Oh, I've made enough films to get my credentials in the film industry. And I've earned enough money to keep the giant house afloat. Which means that I still owe Feury a lot of money. But he doesn't seem to mind.

In a way, I guess, the diamond field that supported my family in Africa has simply been shifted to the glitter of the big screen in America. But through it all, my mother seems to be correct: Behind what is happening is God's care for us. That is the reason I will always dedicate my work: Soli Deo Gloria, "To God alone is the glory."